Three Plays

Walter E. Ledwith

Three Plays
Copyright © 2023 by Walter E. Ledwith
ISBN: 978-1-970153-45-3
Distribution: Ingram Book Company

La Maison Publishing, Inc.
Vero Beach, Florida
The Hibiscus City
lamaisonpublishing@gmail.com

Forward

Those familiar with my work will recognize *'Clichés.'* Having grown fond of the characters in this vignette, I expanded the one act play to three. I hope you enjoy my brief excursion into *'Why the homeless prefer to be homeless.'*

Table of Contents

Triptych

Characters

<u>Arius.</u> Tall, early forties, wearing a trench coat. A good-looking fellow with a con-man's smile. He carries a knapsack on his shoulder. He is a wanderer.

<u>St. Cloud.</u> Mid-height, fifties, deep-set eyes, balding, dressed in a poorly fitting black suit brought to life by a bright green tie. He carries a blanket and a water jug. He is Arius's travel companion.

<u>Albrecht.</u> Dwarf-like man with long hair and a beard. He wears baggy pants and a vest that barely covers his hairy torso.

<u>Anthony Regan.</u> Thirty- something, meticulously dressed, looks as though he just stepped off a yacht. He carries a loaf of bread and a chicken.

<u>Jeffrey.</u> Anthony's assistant. Thin, wears glasses, dressed much like Anthony.

Two security guards.

Guide with two search dogs.

<u>George.</u> A busty, tall, thin girl with brown hair and a black mustache. She has a page-boy haircut and is wearing green fatigues that fail to disguise her gender.

Cliches

Act One

(Leaving a railroad tunnel stage left, Arius and St. Cloud enter, following the track. There is another tunnel stage right. Arius has a knapsack on his shoulder. St. Cloud carries a blanket and water jug.)

Arius: I am hoping to achieve the enlightened state of ambivalence.

St. Cloud: Be careful what you wish for.

Arius: Bliss is when you don't give a crap about anything.

St. Cloud: Best thing since sliced bread.

Arius: Bet your bottom dollar. You're totally free to stop and think about something . . . or move on.

St. Cloud: (nodding his head in agreement) The best of all possible worlds.

Arius: Goes without saying. That's why I chose the life of a mendicant.

St. Cloud: You mean a hobo?

Arius: A voyeur unto life . . . an explorer, an examiner — except for one's own life, of course. Unattached, unencumbered, free to turn your back on the world and follow your heart.

St. Cloud: I watch myself like a frog watches a fly.

Arius: Free and easy.

St. Cloud: Free as a bird?

Arius: Fresh as a daisy.

St. Cloud: If we're so free, how come we have to keep moving?

Arius: Rolling stones gather no moss.

St. Cloud: But suppose the road ends?

Arius: The suppose ta's never arrive and are usually lies. Who knows what tomorrow will bring? . . . Buddha was a mendicant. So was Jesus.

St. Cloud: You're not them.

Arius: And they'll never be me!

St. Cloud: I won't hold it against them.

Arius: I too (*pointing to the sky*) will do something great! Bigger than Socrates! More powerful than Charlie Chaplin or Dr. Phil!

St. Cloud: All I ever wanted was a dog and pony show.

Arius: And a dog and pony show you shall have. The finest! If P.T. Barnum could do it, so can you. . . . Just think small!

St. Cloud: Stop poking your finger in the sky's eye.

Arius: Oops (*looking up*) sorry sky. You never said. How did you ever get a name like St. Cloud?

St. Cloud: I think it was the name of the lady who made out my birth certificate. I can't be sure.

Arius: What about your mother and father?

St. Cloud: They changed their name to fit mine, so . . . no problem.

Arius: Don't take any wooden nickels, my friend—

St. Cloud: No one's ever offered.

Arius: As it should be. . . . Ah! This looks like a good place to camp.

St. Cloud: Until a train comes by. I prefer the highway.

Arius: Not here, (*pointing*) in the clearing over there. Look . . . already we have a fire pit and a log for a pillow. Who could ask for more?

St. Cloud: Until a train comes . . . (*pacing*) then all hell breaks loose. (*He becomes excited as he speaks*) The earth trembles and convulses. The roar of the train grows to be demons escaping from the underworld. (*He puts up his hands to protect his head*) You pull your blanket over your head, hoping the apocalypse will pass. When it does, you try to get back to sleep, and just when your body relaxes, another train steamrolls through your nervous system and you're a wreck again. By morning, you've developed spasms.

Arius: An existential nightmare. We'll make the best of an unpleasant situation.

St. Cloud: I'd rather have ear plugs.

Arius: Ah, . . . man's best friend. Pull up a chair. I'll fill the teakettle. St. Cloud, tonight we feast on an epicurean delight …pork and beans.

St. Cloud: A pig in a poke?

Arius: Beats a can of worms.

St. Cloud: Not without bread to soak up the gravy.

Arius: Man does not live by bread alone!

St. Cloud: It'd be nice to have a bit once in a while, that's all.

Arius: As luck would have it, (*reaching into his trench coat pocket*) I was able to rescue a half loaf of Wonder Bread from a dumpster we passed back at the crossroads.

St. Cloud: The luck of the Irish! God bless the man who invented dumpsters. Garbage in — garbage out, feast or famine.

Arius: Well said stout fellow; give and take, share and share alike and all that.

St. Cloud: (*reaching into his pocket*) And I will bring biscotti to the banquet.

Arius: I thought I saw you skulking around the picnic tables in the park when I used the bathroom there. (*sternly*) Did anyone see you?

St. Cloud: I don't believe so. They were all down by the lake. (*he starts a fire*) Carpe diem! . . . All's fair in love and war.

Arius: Ya' gotta' do what ya' gotta' do. Cut and dried. (*putting the beans into the pot and filling the kettle with water*) It's Darwinian! The survival of the misfits.

St. Cloud: They didn't miss it, otherwise I would have had a knuckle sandwich by now.

Arius: Yet another reason to keep moving.

St. Cloud: It's the law of the jungle . . . while the cat's away the —

Arius: Yes, yes, the wisdom of the ages. I say, . . . is that Albrecht coming from the tunnel?

St. Cloud: Yes, and he appears to have tied one on. He's tighter than a drum.

Arius: Three sheets to the wind. . . . Sit perfectly still. Maybe he won't notice us.

St. Cloud: (*wrapping themselves in the blanket*) Like two peas in a pod.

Arius: (*in a loud whisper*) He sees the fire. He's coming this way.

St. Cloud: He's looking for his ring. They say it was forged in fire.

Arius: He doesn't see us, or the food . . . I hope he doesn't knock everything over.

St. Cloud: He's poking the fire, looking for the ring.

Arius: Listen!!! He's grumbling something.
(from underneath the blanket, they both lean forward to listen)

Albrecht: Where are you? *(wiping tears from his eyes, he returns to the tracks to continue his trek.)*

Arius: *(with a sigh)* He looks like a world-weary cave dweller, walking through the shadows of time.

St. Cloud: They say his relatives were all dwarfs.

Arius: That's pretty old.

St. Cloud: Maybe even older!

Arius: Better late than never—

St. Cloud: Only time will tell.

Arius: And time is of the essence!

St. Cloud: Bah, it's the spitting image of yesterday. Let's eat already!

Arius: Now we're cooking. Seize the day, as you say. Sit . . . I'm happy to serve *(reaching into the other pocket of his trench coat)* and from the very same dumpster I have procured Earl Grey's Deluxe for our evening tea.

St. Cloud: Who has it better than us?

Arius: Ah! *(hand to his ear)* my Muse beckons. We have some things we wanna run by ya'.

St. Cloud: That can't be good. The less said, the better. For all intents and purposes, explaining things is a last-ditch effort to —

Arius: Please allow me my moment in the sun, or in this case, the fire. My hour upon the stage, my fifteen minutes of fame. Hear my bid for glory.

St. Cloud: Okay. Just don't talk fast while I eat. I get confused.

Arius: Words and ideas are like rivers and streams. They all flow from dreams (*stirring the pot*) and beans. Both, food for the soul.

St. Cloud: Now you're a poet?

Arius: With imagination! we create the world.

St. Cloud: With imagination you describe the world. It has nothing to do with what's really there.

Arius: A trifling detail. We are on to better things. Call the hounds and join the hunt for new ideas.

St. Cloud: You're running in circles.

Arius: Of course I am. I'm looking to square things, ya' know. It's the only way —

St. Cloud: Beware! The road to hell is paved with good intentions.

Arius: And so is the road to heaven, so how ya' gonna' know which is which?

St. Cloud: Oh well, that's a topic best discussed after dessert and a couple of brandies. All's well that ends well. . . . How are you gonna get people to listen to these new ideas?

Arius: I will simply point out to them that I don't make mistakes, and that they should put their trust in my record and my accomplishments.

St. Cloud: You don't do nothin', how can you make mistakes? What accomplishments? It's all talk, no action.

Arius: What! (*pacing*) So now you're gonna start breaking cookies?

St. Cloud: If I have to. It's a dirty job, but somebody's got to do it. What mistakes haven't you made? (*Arius pokes the fire as he talks*)

Arius: Well, . . . we have been in Florida for six months and there hasn't been an earthquake. Not a single avalanche. Just as I predicted.

St. Cloud: And the wind-up is?

Arius: When the world is troubled, you gotta learn to dance.

St. Cloud: Now you sound like Lawrence Welk.

Arius: A hero amongst heroes. Trip the lights fantastic!

St. Cloud: A Fandango might be appropriate. I believe I have a pair of castanets in my bag.

Arius: You never cease to amaze me. I could have sworn you were a 'pas de deux' man.

St. Cloud: Still water runs deep.

(*They both dance around the fire. St. Cloud playing the castanets and Arius using the blanket as a cape, twirling it in the air*)

Arius: Where did ya' learn that fancy footwork?

St. Cloud: In a cantina, in Tijuana. How 'bout you?

Arius: I took some LSD at a rock concert outside Toledo. It made such an impression on me, my muscle memory kicks in whenever I hear music. I've become a slave to Terpsichore. I live to serve the muse.

St. Cloud: Not unexpected!

Arius: Let it be known (*emphatically pointing to the sky while dancing*) ... I am a thespian . . . and there are things that only thespians can say. I subscribe to that privilege, and shall avail myself of it. I shall darn the Phrygian Cap.

St. Cloud: Like the court jester.

Arius: ACH! How many nights have I wept with Rigoletto (sic)?

St. Cloud: It's the price we pay for our rebellious natures.

(*Arius sits on the log and stokes the fire*)

Arius: I've got to do something. My life as a lounge lizard didn't pan out. It came to nothing.

St. Cloud: (*sitting next to Arius, arm around his shoulder*) Loud music is rarely harmonious Arius. You're better off being a mendicant.

Arius: (*Jumping up*) Truer words have never been spoken. I will continue as a savant and try to save the world from itself. The blind leading the blind through blood, sweat, and tears.

St. Cloud: I, for one, am willing to invest everything I own in your new idea.

Arius: Thank you St. Cloud, that means a lot to me.

St. Cloud: So, when are we going to start? (rubbing his hands together)

Arius: Well, I have to make plans and all —

St. Cloud: That's what you said last year!

Arius: (*warming his hands over the fire*) Good planning, good execution, make for good results!

St. Cloud: It's déjà vu all over again. Same old, same old. Before we go any further, what's this new idea about?

Arius: It's all about the power of cliches. I want to help people to understand that all they need to know is ensconced in the cliches they use every day. And they are great mnemonic devices as well. You take a bunch of facts, wrap them in a cliché like a burrito, . . . and you have it all in a nutshell.

St. Cloud: Imagine that . . . cliches and burritos, who'd a evva thunk. When do we get started?

Arius: You've already asked that question. You're only allowed to ask a question once. Got it?

St. Cloud: I believe so. When will you begin being a wise mendicant?

Arius: I'm going to sleep on it tonight. John the squirrel told me there are opportunities in Cincinnati for lounge lizards, and somehow or other, I have developed an urge for alligator boots.

St. Cloud: They do make everything electric.

Arius: Yes, but Cincinnati, this time of year, I don't know?

St. Cloud: Any time of year! Last time we were in Cincinnati, I spent the night in jail.

Arius: A case of mistaken identity.

St. Cloud: You told the police I was you!

Arius: I got you out, come morning!

St. Cloud: By promising to leave town before sunrise. We may not be welcome there I think.

Arius: Things to consider. I'll sleep on it.

St. Cloud: You do, do that well.

Arius: Thank you, St. Cloud. Now, are you going to give me a part of the blanket?

St. Cloud: (grudgingly) When are you going to get your own blanket?

Arius: When yours falls apart.

St. Cloud: Just as I had suspected! All you have ever wanted was half of my blanket.

Arius: I will always refuse the whole of it. It wouldn't be the same without you.

St. Cloud: Whatever! *(he leans his head on the log, pulling the blanket to his chin in a fetal position)* It's your turn for fire watch tonight.

Arius: As you wish. Goodnight St. Cloud. *(he stretches out, rests his head on the log, covers himself with the blanket which only reaches his knees.)* This pillow smells like farts.

St. Cloud: You were sitting on it while you were talking. Just your run-of-the-mill brain farts. Go to sleep Arius.

(The train will pass three times during the night. Stage time, one minute between. During the quiet intervals, Arius will awake and tend to the fire. He sleeps through the roar of the train passing as St.

Cloud has spasms underneath the blanket. After the third train, with the sun rising back stage, Arius prepares the morning tea. He takes two stale biscuits from his pocket and places them on a grate on top of the kettle to heat them. St. Cloud pokes his head out from under his covering to see if the coast is clear and it is safe to reenter the world. He checks several times, recoils into a tight ball and springs from under his blanket.)

St. Cloud: I am ready to begin the day.

(St. Cloud circles the fire, trying to appease his cramped muscles. He stops at the cardinal points of the compass to shake off a spasm or two, then continues around the hearth. Arius tends to the fire and kettle.)

Arius: What's that you're doing? You're making me dizzy!

St. Cloud: I'm walking off my spasms.

Arius: Well, walk somewhere else will yah. My head is spinning. You don't me want to fall into the fire . . . or do you?

St. Cloud: Of course not . . . (he gives each leg a good shake) Two minutes I've been awake, and already you're complaining.

Arius: You're right St. Cloud, I'm sorry . . . it's my Anhedonia[1] flaring up again. I will think of more pleasant things and ease the stress. Here, come, sit and have a biscuit. It will more than make up for my rudeness.

(St. Cloud has periodic spasms as they sit on the log with their tea and biscuits)

St. Cloud: Pleasure is stress too, yah know. (*mouth full*)

---

[1] The inability to feel pleasure.

Arius: Yes . . . and the Amygdala demands both pleasure and pain. As it was written, so it shall be —

(*Arius pauses, deep in thought. St. Cloud, waiting for Arius to finish what he was saying, gets up and gives each of his legs a shake and sits down again*)

St. Cloud: Stop screaming.

Arius: I didn't say a word —

St. Cloud: The silence is deafening.

Arius: I'll try to keep it down.

St. Cloud: Please do, you'll wake the neighbors. So what's it gonna' be? What has sleep decided for us today? . . . because I'm not going to Cincinnati —

Arius: Neither am I. I think I'll continue with my plan for changing the world.

St. Cloud: So you're not satisfied with the sun, the moon, the stars. The flowers, the Ocean, the —

Arius: No, no, no, they're okay. It's the percepts I'm after. Change the percepts — you change the thinking. A faulty 'a priori' creates false dichotomies, which create twisted percepts and causes humanity to walk with a limp. We will begin there, and rid ourselves of our braces.

St. Cloud: (*approvingly*) That sounds Phrygian, very Phrygian.

Arius: I got it from a guy who lived in a wine jar in Athens.[2] He was a mendicant too.

---

[2] Diogenes the Cynic

St. Cloud: I'm impressed. . . . But people seem to like these 'a priori'.

Arius: There ya' go again. Must you always be negative? . . . It never ends. To those people I would say, to each his own, because water seeks its own level and there ain't no changing that.

St. Cloud: Then why do we have to do anything at all?

Arius: Point taken . . . but the journey of a thousand miles begins with a single step, so, (*Gesturing*) we must be on our way.

St. Cloud: What's your hurry? You're always in a hurry.

Arius: There's a lot to do.

St. Cloud: There's always a lot to do. But we don't do anything!

Arius: It takes just as long to do nothing as it takes to do something, and it is often the more difficult. (*Arius packs the pot and kettle into his knapsack. St. Cloud folds his blanket and throws it over his shoulder, water jug in hand. They enter the tracks.*) Now, where was I?

St. Cloud: Cliches and burritos.

Arius: Yes! And what to do with them!

St. Cloud: Ideas have always been marketable.

Arius: And we're on the silk road. (*stopping in front of the tunnel*) I will be a guiding light.

St. Cloud: Well, shine a little light this way will yah! . . .We should go, NOTHING is waiting for us. (*they disappear into the tunnel and continue talking, now with an echo*)

Arius: Yes, of course. As I was saying, a good cliché is worth a thousand words!

St. Cloud: I avoid them like the plague.

Curtain

Sciamachy

Act Two

(Arius and St. Cloud exit a railroad tunnel, stage right, following the tracks. A water tower is seen in the distance. The stage is outlined with trees and thicket, with railroad tracks passing through. Downstage, is a campsite with a tripod over a fire pit and two chairs made from the surrounding trees. Rustic thrones with high backs that swallow up its occupants.)

Arius: I will not rest until I put Sciamachy in its place!

St. Cloud: (pointing back at the tunnel) But you just said, on the other side, that you were going to devote yourself to educating the world as to the importance of clichés. A revolution, remember . . . burritos, a better world, yada-yada.

Arius: That was ages ago. We've moved on.

St. Cloud: Yah, seventeen minutes and one tunnel ago.

Arius: The revolution will have to wait! How do you know it's been seventeen minutes?

St. Cloud: (with both thumbs up) The sun.

Arius: Persistent fellow that sun . . . appearing-disappearing, can't make up his mind. (shaping his hands to form binoculars) Look, someone is sleeping in the bushes.

St. Cloud: (walking over to take a look) It's Albrecht.

Arius: How do you know?

St. Cloud: I can smell him.

Arius: You must have a file cabinet of smells in that brain of yours.

St. Cloud: It's one of my default systems. My nose-brain, my "Rhinencephalon."

Arius: Listening to you always makes me want to get down on all fours to forage.[3]

St. Cloud: Necessary to live life more completely.

Arius: Completely absorbed maybe.

---

[3] Letter : Voltaire to Rousseau

St. Cloud: I don't have anything else to do.

Arius: But I do! These imaginary enemies are consuming all my energy. They are puppeteers pulling my strings. Every time I start off in one direction, they pull me in another.

St. Cloud: We should go.

Arius: I have to resolve this Sciamachy business. I can't get anything done . . . look! *(Binoculars again)* Up ahead, there's a campsite. Perfect . . . let's make camp.

St. Cloud: It's only seven minutes past noon. We've just started!

Arius: I can't go any further until I get this business straight.

(They enter the campsite to find two large chairs and a bench around a fire pit. Delighted, they both sink into the chairs. The arm rests sit high on their torso so both men are sitting low with raised arms.)

Arius: *(surveying the area)* Others have made this journey before us. Travelers, like ourselves, on the road to forever.

St. Cloud: Big people! . . . The armrests here are clear to my shoulders.

Arius: That's done purposely. The idea is, as you contemplate the universe, your arms are raised to gather in new things. You know, putting the body into the equation. The Harley Davidson rider reaps the same effect.

St. Cloud: I suppose I could get used to it. Sitting like this, there's little else you can do but to contemplate the universe.

Arius: Exactly the intention of the builders! This is a transporting vehicle that will take us to distant ports, yet to be named.

St. Cloud: Let's get on with it then. Maybe we can finish before dinner.

Arius: Good man! We have some thought problems to solve.

St. Cloud: (*hands fidgeting*) We can't stay, you know . . . we have no food.

Arius: We can't leave? . . . this could be groundbreaking.

St. Cloud: (*annoyed*) We can't stay here! We have no food! We're in the middle of nowhere. There's not a diner for miles.

Arius: So, you would rather eat at a trough than dine alfresco, here, in this wonderful setting, (*waving his hands*) in this land of transition.

St. Cloud: Once again, we have no food.

Arius: Something will come up.

St. Cloud: Before the sun goes down, I hope. You have to be near food in order to eat it.

Arius: Oh 'ye of little faith.' (*Arius gets up and begins pacing, hands behind his back, circling the fire pit clockwise*) Would it be so terrible to miss a meal? You could afford to lose a few pounds, my friend.

St Cloud: (*on his feet, hands behind his back, circles the firepit counter-clockwise*) You are not to comment on my weight. We agreed. You gave your word. Where are your manners?

Arius: The truth doesn't have any manners. Manners are an avoidance of the obvious. While we're at it . . . you need a haircut.

St. Cloud: I only have ten hairs on my head and I'm not cutting any of them.

Arius: How do you know there are only ten?

St. Cloud: I counted them at the last gas station we were at . . . when I was at my toilet. I have ten hairs and three new sprouts.

Arius: Humm (*hand to chin*) a comb and brush set may be necessary the next time we celebrate the day of your birth . . . You know, I think you should grow a mustache as well. It would bring out the color of your eyes.

St. Cloud: A mustache would make me look fat. And my eyes have no color to bring out. They are transparent cordate binoculars.

Arius: Yes, heart-shaped binoculars, that's what makes you stand out.

St. Cloud: It runs in the family. You can see clear through to my brain. I thought everybody was like that until I went to kindergarten. My parents never told me I was different and I grew up thinking everyone had translucent eyes, but that's another story.

Arius: A story begging to be told, I sense . . . Listen (*cupping his hand to his ear*) someone is coming. Quick! To the chairs. Act like this place is our home.

(*Anthony enters from inside the tunnel. He is carrying a loaf of bread under his arm and a chicken in his other hand. He appears confused and disorientated.*)

Arius: Act like you don't see him.

St. Cloud: I smell food!

Arius: Shush! Quiet.

Anthony: Hello there! Hello!

Arius: Hello yourself.

St. Cloud: Who are you? What's that you have there in your hands?

Anthony: It's about all I've got in the world. A loaf of bread and a stewing chicken. I hope I haven't interrupted anything important.

Arius: Of course you have, but sit anyway, take a load off. (*With a sweeping gesture*) Welcome to this place –'me casa, su casa.'

Anthony: Yes, yes, thank you. (*sitting on the bench, confused*) Even if only for a little while.

Arius: What brings you to our humble domicile?

Anthony: I feel as though I have left a dark tunnel and have entered the light.

St. Cloud: You have.

Anthony: Ah! That explains it.

Arius: In more ways than one. You have entered the realm of the adept.

St. Cloud: Or the 'Theater of the Ridiculous.'

Arius: Fate has brought you here for a reason and we are willing to help you. For a small remuneration, of course.

St. Cloud: (*sniffing the air*) Just a small one.

Anthony: Your hospitality is most welcome, though I have little to offer.

St. Cloud: You have all the riches a man could hope for.

Arius: And then some. And, you are here because?

Anthony: Last I remember, I was arguing with my wife. I have been wandering ever since.

Arius: Details please.

Anthony: Well, we were grocery shopping at that high-end market outside town. The over-priced, boring one you have to dress for.

St. Cloud: You dress up to go shopping?

Anthony: Of course, the neighbors, you know. Anyway, we argued, she lost it, and on the way home my one and only drove me into the wilderness and parked. She reached into the back, grabbed a loaf of bread and threw it at me. Then grabbed a chicken from the bag and shoved it in my chest. "Get out!" she yelled and drove off in a cloud of dust. I remember little else but for a dark tunnel that echoed my footsteps . . . and a light in the distance.

Arius: What was the argument about?

Anthony: Restless leg syndrome . . . I have restless leg syndrome.

Arius: Well, St. Cloud, you have someone to dance with next time a train passes by.

Anthony: It's all very confusing.

St. Cloud: Nothing that can't be sorted out after a good meal.

Anthony: I have a chicken and a loaf of bread here.

St Cloud: So, you do. How do you like that! I'm sure we can put something together.

Anthony: (*looking into the pit*) There's no wood or even ashes in the firepit. . . . Looks like it hasn't been used for a while.

Arius: We've been fasting. Sit back. Relax. (*Rising from his chair, taking the victuals from Anthony, giving them to St. Cloud*) St. Cloud will take care of it all.

Anthony: I wouldn't want to impose. You have been very gracious, inviting me into your home.

Arius: It's what we do. Consider it a mutual gift giving. We offer a safe place for you to repose yourself and you reciprocate with the offering of your victuals as recompense for our welcome.

St. Cloud: A paradigm for human society since the time of Homer.

Arius: Welcome noble traveler! (*bowing at the waist*)

Anthony: Can't argue with that, (*looking at his empty hands, rubbing his knees*) given the circumstances.

(*St. Cloud puts the bounty in his chair, removes a jug of water from his satchel. Arius takes the cooking pot from his bag and hands it to St. Cloud, who puts the chicken in the pot and sets it on the tripod. They both stare at it, confused.*)

Arius: There's no fire. You can't cook a chicken without fire.

St. Cloud: Of course! I've got to get some wood for the fire. Be right back. (*running off stage*)

Anthony: (*calling after him*) Is there anything I can do to help?

Arius: No, no, you just sit back and relax. You're a guest! St. Cloud is a master chef and soon you will be sopping his chicken gravy with that wonderful wheat bread you've brought. I say, who has it better than us?

Albrecht: (*who has been sleeping in the bushes, sits up*) I hear voices. (*awkwardly getting to his feet, looking around, hand to his ear*) They're not far away. (*walking towards the voices, talking to himself*) Sure is getting crowded around here lately. (*seeing them, he runs to the fire pit and searches it. Not finding anything, he stands and looks into the pot, seeing the chicken*) There's no fire. You can't cook a chicken without a fire!

Arius: Well, hello to you too, Albrecht. Welcome to our humble home.

Albrecht: (*looking into his face*) Do I know you? Maybe. Oh, it's you . . . where's your know-it-all friend? The short guy with the noisy tie. I've never seen you without him before.

Arius: He's off to fetch some firewood.

Albrecht: (*sitting on the bench next to Anthony, extending his hand*) Hello, I'm Albrecht. I'm a traveler.

Anthony: Glad to meet you Mr. Albrecht. My name is Anthony and I'm on the board of directors of several corporations.

Albrecht: Okay . . . if you say so (*turning to Arius*) He didn't need to do that. There's a pile of firewood over there behind the hedges.

Arius: Oh, . . . he must have forgotten. Not to worry, he can add the new wood to the pile.

(*Albrecht gets up and goes to the hedge where the woodpile is and returns with an armful. He arranges the wood in the firepit and takes a box of stick matches from his vest pocket and starts a fire*)

Anthony: So Arius, have you been living here long?

Arius: Oh, it's been a while I guess. Time passes and you know, one loses track . . . but all of this wasn't built in a day.

Anthony: Mr. Albrecht, can I help in any way? (*Albrecht ignores him.*) That's a wonderful fire. At the very least, you must stay for dinner. That is if it's alright with you Arius?

Arius: (*staring down Albrecht*) Of course . . . Albrecht is always welcome.

Albrecht: **(***confused, getting into Arius's face)* Are you sure I know you? Oh, yah . . . you're with the noisy tie. You look different with your arms in the air. Then I will stay, and even contribute to this evening's supper. (*He reaches into his pants pocket*) I have a turnip and, (*reaching deep into his other pocket*) a large onion for the pot.

Arius: It just gets better and better . . . and look, St. Cloud is back. St. Cloud, we forgot about the wood stashed behind the hedge.

St. Cloud: (*seeing the fire already set up, drops an arm full of wood behind his chair, rushes to sit in it.*) So we did. I remember now. No one sits in my chair, Albrecht. (*flipping his tie at him*)

Arius: Albrecht was good enough to contribute a turnip and an onion to our banquet and he has helped with the fire.

St. Cloud: (*standing, reaching into his pocket*) I will raise you one Russet potato, and (*pouring the last of the water from the jug, exasperated*) we're out of water!

Arius: (*surprised*) You never cease to amaze me. A large russet potato? And you wanted to forsake this feast with some mawkish excuse for nourishment at a —

Albrecht: (*taking the jug from St. Cloud*) There's a water tower just down the track, I'll get some. (*walking the track off stage*)

Arius: St. Cloud, you look upset.

St. Cloud: He drives the olfactory to madness.

Anthony: Does he work for you? He seems to know more about your house than you do.

Arius: Humm . . . something to consider. But with our schedule and all —

St. Cloud: Yes, our busy schedule prohibits our taking on servants. (*Albrecht returns with the water. St Cloud grabs it from him and adds water to the pot.*) There can only be one chef in this kitchen! (*Albrecht returns to the bench, folds his hands in his lap. St. Cloud returns to his chair, placing his arms on the armrests*)

Arius: (*looking into the pot*) Amazing! (*begins pacing around the circle*) While we are waiting on the victuals, perhaps we can enter upon some noetic musings. What say you . . . we start with sciamachy. An inquiry we've begun just this morning.

Albrecht: What kinda word is skee mariachi?

Arius: Oh, I don't know . . . one with a meaning I can tell you.

Anthony: It's Greek. Skia is shadow and machy is to fight. Fighting shadows or imaginary enemies.

St. Cloud: Like Don Quixote.

Anthony: Exactly.

Albrecht: Sounds made up to me.

St. Cloud: Of course it's made up, doofus. All words are made up. Their meanings too.

Arius: Eyes here people. Let's stay focused. We'll get lost if we don't follow the moderator.

Albrecht: How do you know? Did you ever try?

Arius: Try what?

Albrecht: To get lost. Lose focus. Not follow the moderator.

Arius: No need to try. I know what the result would be. That's why I'm always focused.

Albrecht: How do you know if you never tried?

Arius: It's implied.

Albrecht: Says who?

Arius: Stop this. I'm losing my concentration. You're beginning to sound like St. Cloud.

St. Cloud: Don't compare me to this malodorous vagabond!

Anthony: I don't smell a thing. Deviated septum you know … since childhood.

Albrecht: (*standing, preening himself*) It's a new fragrance. It came with my new vest. (*proudly showing it off*). I found it in a Goodwill box in South Philly.

St. Cloud: Close to the stockyards, I'd say.

Albrecht: A redolence,[4] with just a hint of the beast.

Arius: Enough! . . . now gentlemen, to continue. I have come to the conclusion that sciamachy affects each of us . . . perhaps in different ways, but it remains . . . we're all affected.

Albrecht: Not me. All my enemies are all too real.

Anthony: I have an example. It's rather personal though.

Arius: (*sitting in his chair, arms raised*) Continue, please.

Anthony: Lately, as soon as I lay my head down on the pillow, these thoughts . . . these accusations come nonstop and they

---

[4] Redolence: Pleasant bouquet or fragrance

hound me all night. Every sin. Every cross word spoken, every victim of my insensitivity parades themselves across the big screen in my mind. I want to run. It causes a spasm in my leg. When I look in the mirror, the person I see is not anyone I know.

Albrecht: How do ya fight that! You're your own enemy? . . . Why the hell would you want to fight yourself?

Arius: (*ignoring Albrecht*) Anthony, do you sense an entity controlling the pictures in your mind?

St. Cloud: Guilty conscious maybe?

Albrecht: Look at him. He looks like he's on his way to a Sunday dinner. What could he be guilty of?

St. Cloud: The same things as you or I.

Albrecht: (*surprised, then scrutinizing Anthony*) You beast!

Arius: Are the pictures random or do they appear in a specific order?

Anthony: They're random. And always with a recrimination about how I could have done better.

Arius: And does this recriminator always speak with the same voice?

St. Cloud: I love that word . . . Recriminator —

Albrecht: What's it mean?

St. Cloud: Shush! (finger to his lips)

Albrecht: What does shush mean?

St. Cloud: Stop talking.

Albrecht: No, I want to know what shush means.

St. Cloud: It means to stop talking, you —

Arius: Quiet! Now, Anthony, does this happen every night?

Anthony: No, it comes and goes, sometimes for a week at a time. After that, I sleep like a baby. Until they reappear.

St. Cloud: What about the good stuff you've done? Do you see the pictures of that? Maybe with an 'atta boy'?

Anthony: No, just the nasty stuff.

Arius: So, your demon is a tormenting torturer. (*pacing clockwise around fire pit*) Okay, now we're getting somewhere.

St. Cloud: (*getting up, stirring the pot, then pacing counterclockwise*) I say it's not invisible enemies at all. It's your somatosensory system telling you there's something wrong and in need of correction. Telling you to pay attention —

Arius: Pay attention to what? No, no. Anthony, you have an otherwise idyllic life. I think it's demons, creating havoc with your spirit.

Anthony: It's true. I want for nothing . . . I'm free to do whatever I choose. . . . (to Albrecht) Often I think I'm the luckiest man on the face of the earth. It's all been given to me, everything I own.

Albrecht: The only thing you own is the breath in your lungs, and even that, not for long. . . . You're making up problems. You don't have any, so you're making them up.

St. Cloud: (*sliding into his chair, arms raised*) The somatosensory system is the starship that carries you through space. This skin that covers our bones is one big antenna. It measures the temperature, the light, . . . friend and foe on the horizon. The eyes filter out all that is not relevant to our little world. The ears are constantly surveying the landscape. One giant antenna collecting data and sending it to the central command center at the Solar Plexus. And what about the brain, you ask? Switching centers is all it is. That's how your legs know to move when you come across a bear in the woods. All the right switches are thrown and you get the hell out of there.

Arius: (returning to his chair) This coming from a man who admits being nose-brain dominant.

St. Cloud: That's my take on the matter.

Anthony: And here I thought the somatosensory system was about homeostasis.

Albrecht: (gets up to stir the pot and is shooed away by St. Cloud. He circles the firepit as he talks) All of this talk is only good for driving yourself crazy. Right now is the best it's ever been . . . for everyone. (he stops in front of Anthony) You say you have a charmed life, well so do we all. This is a world full of abundance, and it's all there waiting for us. (Continues in his circle around the fire pit, using his hands to punctuate what he's saying) When I want to take a lady out for a romantic dinner, I have my pick of the best restaurants. There's a dumpster for every occasion. If she wants Chinese, I take her to the Golden Pheasant. If it's Italian she craves, there is the menu at Momma Marotta's Trattoria, my personal favorite. She uses only the finest ingredients, has the best wine and always plays romantic music. She serves sizeable portions, so there's always plenty in the dumpster. I set a couple of cardboard boxes by the window. (facing the audience framing a camera shot with his hands, with a narrator's voice) The music finds us on a warm summer's night. Roses, discarded by the florist down the street, scent the air. A borrowed towel from a clothes line provides the tablecloth and the table is set. (he continues walking) A warm and welcoming ambience. . . . Who could ask for more? After dinner we might stroll to the outskirts of the city to watch the light show in the sky. This time of year, Orion is doing a slow dance across the stage. There is a different show every night, free of charge, for all who wish to indulge. *(he sits down next to Anthony)*

St. Cloud: This coming from a man who scours firepits along railroad tracks, looking for a lost ring.

Albrecht: It's not a ring. Everybody gets that wrong, it's a bracelet, not a ring. And I have no idea where the forged in fire came from. It was a gift and it's very special to me. It's been seven years I have been searching, so I'm sure to find it soon.

Arius: Moving right along people, let's stay focused.

St Cloud: **(***to Albrecht)* A gift from whom?

Albrecht: My mother, if you must know.

Arius: Focus people . . . we have to stay focused. None of this is helping us find Anthony's invisible enemies.

Albrecht: *(folding his arms)* They're invisible because they don't exist.

St. Cloud: It's the somatosensory command center telling ya' there's something wrong. Like when you're hungry and you don't have anything to eat. Fear sets in and takes control of the body, causing a torturous panic.

Arius: *(pacing again)* Where do they live, these minions of anxiety? Do they consult each other? Is there a particular percept that stages the sciamachy? What are they? They're not real. They don't exist in the here and now or anyplace else except maybe our muscles. They're holograms. Holograms of what once existed.

St. Cloud: Maybe we should let it rest.

Arius: We all spend a good part of our life fighting these imaginary enemies, so it behooves us to find out what's going on. Maybe the somatosensory system does activate it. I was so hoping for a rousing exorcism . . . but, we have to move on.

Anthony: It's all so thick. I'm even more confused than before. (*getting up to stir the pot*) Ah, the meat is falling off the bone. I think our stew is done. But it's only been . . . how did it cook so fast?

(Arius digs into his knapsack and retrieves two mess-kits and utensils. Albrecht takes hot sauce from his pocket, holds it in his hands as he waits.)

St. Cloud: What's that?

Albrecht: Hot sauce. And its very hot. Guaranteed to clear the sinuses. I drink it right from the bottle whenever I'm congested.

Arius: I'm afraid we only have settings for two people.

St. Cloud: Does that mean we should have our first and second portions together?

Arius: Yes, I believe it does. (*explaining to Anthony*) Our dinnerware is at our other house. We're mendicants you know. Peripatetic philosophers[5] bringing our knowledge to the world —

St. Cloud: And it gets messy passing the plates back and forth.

---

[5] Peripatetic philosophers: 'from place to place'. The school of Aristotle, taught while walking in the Lyceum.

Albrecht: (*jumping to his feet, handing the hot sauce to Anthony*) Bullshit! There will be nothing left. I'll be right back. (*he goes to the bush and retrieves two mess kits. St. Cloud grabs the hot sauce and pours some into the stew, then gives it back. Albrecht hands Anthony a mess kit*) Here ya go, problem solved. Now we can all eat together.

Anthony: Excellent! Will the host be serving this evening's fare?

Arius: Yes, yes of course, since I am the only one with a ladle.

Albrecht: I have a ladle.

Arius: You certainly are a resourceful fellow Albrecht, (*under his breath*) considering where we are. . . . Come gather everyone, a feast awaits us. This evening we will indulge in a culinary delight. Help yourself to the bread.

(*Arius serves each of them a portion and they return to their seats. They eat greedily, making grunting sounds.*)

Anthony: When did I develop this voracious appetite?

St. Cloud: It comes with the cuisine.

Albrecht: Want some hot sauce?

Anthony: No thank you.

Arius: My compliments to the chef. This is a meal that's fit for a king.

St. Cloud: And it has the most delicious aroma.

Anthony: It's food for thought! And I've been thinking. You've shown me a different way of seeing things, which I think might be valuable. I'm not going to give up a soft bed for a sleeping bag, but I'd like to follow through with what we've started here. I'd like you to come to work for me as consultants. I say this now because anytime soon my people are going to find me and I wanted your opinion before they arrive.

Albrecht: You have people?

Anthony: Yes, quite a few and I'd like you to join them.

St. Cloud: What would we have to do?

Arius: And what would the emolument be for our services?

Anthony: You will be well paid. With a good many perks too. Your job would be to consult with me and my team on various ongoing problems and projects the corporation is working on. You give us your take and suggestions for the matter at hand, and we add it to our mix. That's all. We'll get you an office, a secretary and anything else you need.

Albrecht: What would I do?

Anthony: You would share with us that quirky up-side-down way you look at things. Together, we might come up with something new and innovative. What do you say? Interested?

St. Cloud: I say I'm ready for a second helping.

(*Albrecht jumps to his place at the fireplace, St. Cloud opposite him.*)

Albrecht: I'll have the bones, with it's sweet juices and succulent marrow.

Arius: (*to Anthony*)Your wife's weaponized chicken has served us well my friend.

Anthony: It certainly has, in so many ways. We will talk more on that later. Right now, I'm hungry.

(*Arius serves each of them a spoon at a time. They examine each other's portions to be sure they are equal. Albrecht's plate holds the carcass of the chicken. They take a slice of bread and return to their seats.)*

Arius: What say you St. Cloud? Are we interested? Are you ready to move to the city?

St. Cloud: We can still work on clichés, and put feathers on sciamachy while we are there.

Anthony: And Albrecht, you can take your ladies inside of the restaurants if you like.

Albrecht: It would depend on the atmosphere of the joint. (*gnawing on a chicken bone*)

Arius: And where would we be relocating to?

Anthony: We have corporate headquarters in Tampa and Cincinnati. We can shuttle back and forth on the company jet.

St. Cloud: Cincinnati! Never!

Arius: Tampa yes, definitely not Cincinnati, no.

St. Cloud: NOoooo.

Anthony: Then Tampa it is.

Albrecht: The train on this line goes right through Tampa.

Anthony: I know, the company owns the railroad.

St. Cloud: So, you're the landlord. I have some quality-of-life issues to take up with you, mister. The noise from the trains is maddening.

Arius: Moving right along. St. Cloud, I say we jump right in and give it a try.

Albrecht: What the hell, I'm game.

St. Cloud: He was talking to me. In answer to your question, yes. No Cincinnati though.

Albrecht: *(echoes of dogs barking come from the tunnel)* Listen …. Do you hear that? They're coming through the tunnel. (*All of them cup their hand to their ears to listen.*) Look, … there are several of them. They're coming this way. (*They form binoculars with their hands.*) We should pack it in.

Arius: Were not moving. I know the landlord personally.

(Anthony's assistant Jeffrey approaches, out of breath and looking haggard.)

Jeffrey: Mr. Regan, at last, we've been searching for you all day. We were very worried. Are you all right? Did these men kidnap you?

Anthony: Jeffrey! I figured you'd be along. Everything is fine. These people are my new friends and soon to be consultants at the 'Tampa' office. Make a note to fire the two pretenders we have in the job now. Did you bring the limo?

Jeffrey: Yes, it's on the other side of the tunnel.

Anthony: Good, we'll need it to get to town. (*to Arius and St. Cloud*) We should pack up gentlemen, so we can be on our way.

(Arius and St. Cloud scurry about gathering their belongings)

Jeffrey, call ahead and have the guest house made ready for our friends. The big one should be good. They will need a staff for the house (*circling the firepit clockwise*) . . . and a secretary. And tell the wife to have three extra places set for dinner. No, better yet, tell Amie, she'll get it done quicker. (*Jeffrey frantically writes everything down*)

Jeffrey: Mr. Regan, you look different. You've changed.

Anthony: I don't know if it's the food, the camaraderie or what, but I have achieved a sudden and unexpected blast of satori. An Epiphany of sorts. An awakening. I have finally come to my majority.

Jeffrey: If you say so, sir. You talk different too.

Anthony: I'm learning to use language to help me parse out meaning. It's a great gift. (pacing) Also, call the Cincinnati office and tell them I will not be at the meeting on Friday but will teleconference with them.

(Albrecht pets the search dogs and scrutinizes the security guards. Arius and St. Cloud have gathered their belongings and join Anthony)

Arius: (whispers to St. Cloud) I told you something would come up.

Anthony: Well gentleman, are we ready to go? (They nod yes.) Great! Jeffrey, (with a bounding gait) let's get started.

(Albrecht buttons his vest, throws his head back and leads the way into the tunnel. The others follow behind. As they enter the tunnel, Arius slips his arm around Anthony's shoulder.)

Arius: Anthony, may I call you Tony? I think I may have some ideas that you might be interested in.

Anthony: How did that chicken cook so fast?

Curtain

The Return

Act Three

(Arius and St. Cloud have returned from their life in the city as advisors to Anthony. Thrilled at first, the good life became less attractive as time went by. The set is the same as in the last scene. Arius and St. Cloud exit the tunnel carrying extra bags; their bounty from the city. Once in the open air they both stop, sigh and smile at each other.)

Arius: Home at last, St. Cloud. Back to a world that is ordered and predictable. A world, though fraught with dangers, is no match for our skills. Ahh! . . . take in that air. That is the fresh air of promise. Away from the madness, the neurosis and the illnesses that come with worry.

St. Cloud: Just being there makes you sick. Through osmosis.

Arius: Epidemics are endemic to large herds.

St. Cloud: The 'They say' have people all confused. The 'consensus of opinion' has incorporated chaos theory into people's lives. Folks are not sure who they are, or where they're going. Whether they are good or bad, on the right side of history or if tomorrow the economy will come crashing down.

Arius: Intentionally so, I dare say. Anxious people are easier to control. How else are you going to convince eight billion people to behave and live orderly lives?

St. Cloud: So, they're using chaos to avert chaos.

Arius: Me thinks so. Have to give them credit, it's a brilliant plan. *(they reach the campsite and relieve themselves of their baggage)* Well, at least it keeps them busy. Otherwise, they'd all be out here trying to muscle in on our world.

St. Cloud: *(circling the pit counter-clockwise)* It drives me to distraction to hear people wherever I go, repeating the same things, in the same word order, over and over again. And the way they live, ach! Like automatons. *(sitting in their chairs)* Doing the same things every day is little more than sleepwalking.

Arius: Sooo Manchurian.

St. Cloud: All in the hope that if they revisit groundhog day enough times they can live the way we do. Answerable only to ourselves, independent and carefree.

Arius: They expected me to bathe three times a day . . . You don't even have the time between baths to get dirty. I'm surprised they have any skin left after all that scrubbing. Imagine?

St. Cloud: They hounded me to change my tie every day . . . and twice on Sundays. Don't they know that would confuse people? How would folks know who they're talking to?

Arius: But the best was when they told Albrecht he had to wear a shirt underneath his vest.

St. Cloud: That would interfere with his 'redolence'. It took years to develop *you* know . . . So I heard him say.

Arius: I wonder what happened to him? One day, he was just gone.

St. Cloud: He's no stranger to the rails, not to worry, he knows where he's going.

Arius: I don't blame him for leaving. There is no challenge to living in a big house filled with servants and lackeys. Everything is too easy. People just acquire the trading object, in this case money, and walk across the street to satisfy their needs.

St. Cloud: I prefer beads.

Arius: (*Ignoring St. Cloud, circling the pit clockwise*) Not like us. You and I awake every morning to a challenge. Our wits and skill allow us to secure our needs. We know not how they will come, or from where, but they will come because we make it so. We avail ourselves of what's available. Foragers on the landscape, like our ancestors before us.

St. Cloud: Shopping is foraging.

Arius: It most certainly is. Foraging is in our DNA. Shopping is just the way the gene expresses itself in the present world. All of our important behaviors are programmed in brilliant chains of DNA. It's how a robin knows how to build a nest or a beaver a dam. There's no schooling, just knowing.

St. Cloud: Oops . . . there goes the individual. (*hand-binoculars*) Swallowed by the crowd. Oh well . . . it had a good run.

Arius: (*sitting down*) Ever since people started writing things down.

St. Cloud: Good riddance! Created quite a few psychopaths I'd say.

Arius: And a land called Isolation.

St. Cloud: (*shaking his head*) Aberrant to nature it is.

Arius: It's the Minotaur's maze. Only the beast understands its logic. Only he knows the way out.

St. Cloud: Should we build a fire?

Arius: Yes. And then wait for the next thing to happen. Like a spider waiting for its web to shake.

St. Cloud: We don't have to wait. Before we left, I packed a bag from the pantry and took a few choice morsels from the freezer.

Arius: Excellent! I grabbed a few of the utensils myself. And what are our menu options for today?

St. Cloud: I have a ham, a turkey breast and a leg of lamb. Slim pickings in the pantry though. Not a single can of 'Goofy's Baked Beans' was there to be found.

Arius: Barbarians.

St. Cloud: They packed the pantry with stuff that rots your teeth.

Arius: A plot, no doubt by the American Dental Association.

St. Cloud: I did manage to scavenge a couple cans of spam—

Arius: Ah, dessert!

St. Cloud: and a few tins of spinach.

Arius: A breakfast favorite, well done! The universe is declaring the world our oyster St. Cloud, *(Albrecht appears from behind the bush with an armful of wood)* and speaking of barbarians, look-see who's coming.

St. Cloud: Ugh! Albrecht. I was afraid we might evoke him, using his name and all.

Arius: Can we un-use his name or something?

St. Cloud: I'll have to look into that.

Albrecht: Gentlemen! *(dropping the wood beside the fire pit)* I was wondering how long it would take you to make it back.

Arius: Hello Albrecht. Thank you. It's good to be home. We were just going to start a fire.

Albrecht: I beat ya to it.

(Arius, with binoculars to his eyes, has a look of horror on his face. St. Cloud sees this and jumps up to see what it is. An apparition with

an arm full of wood comes from the bush and drops its load behind St. Cloud's chair. He jumps into his seat.

St. Cloud: My chair!

George: I suppose these are the friends you talked about. (*turning to go back to the bush*) I'll get the water.

Arius: Well Albrecht, I see you've been a busy man. I mean with your new consort and all.

Albrecht: Yes, and I found my bracelet. (*showing the bracelet on his wrist*) It was in a secret pocket in my pants. I found it when we went skinny dipping in the river.

St. Cloud: After all those years of searching, go figure. Skinny dipping . . . I thought I detected a change of atmosphere in your presence.

Arius: You might think about taking your vest off more often. But continue . . . tell us about your girlfriend?

Albrecht: She's not my girlfriend. She's a man. Her name is George.

St. Cloud: But she is curvy and has big breasts!

Albrecht: True, a lot of her is still a girl. But he's 'not a girl'! (*laughing*) And she's a funny 'not a girl' too. She tells people she's a man transitioning to be a woman.

St. Cloud: She . . . I mean he, does have a mustache.

Albrecht: He-she whatever, I don't care. We've decided to call ourselves "Close."

Arius: And so it shall be. From this moment on we will call you "close" couple.

St. Cloud: Works for me. So where did you two find each other?

Albrecht: In the train yards outside Miami. I'd seen her lounging around for a while and decided to introduce myself. We hit it off right away.

Arius: Of course. 'A Sunday in the park with George'!

St. Cloud: So, (*leaning forward to listen*) what did you talk about?

Albrecht: We didn't talk much. It only gets in the way.

St. Cloud: I won't ask, but . . . in what way?

Albrecht: You're a creepy little man. Do you understand that?

St. Cloud: It's taken years and a lot of hard work to become who I am. And I'll not change a thing.

Albrecht: Nobody's asking you to. The world needs creepy little men. It's not any of my business. You know, I think I'm beginning to like you . . . but I still hate the tie.

(*George has returned with two jugs of water and places them at the fire pit*)

George: Well, I've done my bit.

St. Cloud: Your bit of what?

George: I've brought firewood and water. That gets me some rights. So, what's for dinner?

Arius: So you have, and so you do. You're also 'close', so that makes you family.

George: (*speaking to Albrecht*) You covered a lot of territory in that short amount of time. Sooo, whatever your name is, what's for dinner?

Arius: Oh, I'm sorry. Bad manners on my part. I am Arius and this is St. Cloud.

St. Cloud: We're having turkey spaghetti tonight.

George: Is that the one with turkey and brown gravy mixed in spaghetti. . . . Man, that is good. I had it in Omaha a couple of weeks back. One of my favorites.

St. Cloud: The Omaha camp loves my turkey spaghetti. They didn't want to let us leave.

(*Arius places his pot on the tripod over the fire*)

Arius: We had to sneak out in the middle of the night.

St. Cloud: The price of success. . . . They wanted me to write a 'Travelers Cookbook'. (*pouring water into the pot*) Which of course would be impossible, being closely guarded family secrets and all. (George *sits next to Albrecht on the bench.*)

George: (*accusingly*) Why don't you want to share with other travelers? They're our people. Like family. Travelers communities are intentional communities now. If you don't want to belong, you should just pack up and find another camp.

Arius: We did, under the cloak of darkness.

St. Cloud: (*taking a turkey breast from his bag, mixing ingredients, stirring the pot*) I don't like being told what to do. No matter who's doin' the tellin'. Whatever they call themselves.

Arius: The travelers of former times were livid in their graves. (*circling the pit clockwise*) St. Cloud, I neglected to tell you, and Albrecht, I'm glad you're here. I have good news! We have a camp of our own now. Before we left, Anthony stopped by to say goodbye and gave me paperwork that states we have leased one acre of land east of the tracks for ninety-nine years for one dollar. Right where we're standing. To use whenever we want, and do with whatever we like. This is our land. The three of us.

St. Cloud: (*stirring the food then circling the pit counter clockwise*) That changes everything. I don't know. . . . Is that what we want?

George: Does that mean this gorgeous man is a rich landowner? (*taking Albrecht's hand, whispering*) Soon as we do the transition, I'm gonna marry you.

Albrecht: We could go the courthouse and get married tomorrow. No problem. I know the way 'cause I've been arraigned there a couple of times. And I know the judge. . . . It just wouldn't be a same sex marriage—

George: It would be a lie then. It would be a marriage between a man and a woman and I'm not a woman and neither are you. So it wouldn't be a marriage.

Albrecht: If you say so. (*George drags Albrecht away from the circle to talk.*) It's okay to talk around them--

George: I wanna talk in private.

Arius: (*sitting in his chair*) Me thinks Albrecht is in love.

St. Cloud: Or in heat, look at them. . . . (*stirring*) I don't think she likes us.

Arius: What makes you say that?

St. Cloud: I caught her, him, sneering at us a couple of times.

Arius: In the short time we've known her/him. That's a lot of sneering. Like when you're waiting on line at the post office or something. . . . Perhaps it's her way of showing contentment.

St. Cloud: I don't think so. All of her muscles were tightened up. But who cares anyway.

Arius: Not me.

St. Cloud: Not anyone. Only Albrecht. And now we're tied to it all cause he's our partner. Our good fortune may very well be a curse.

Arius: It's the curse of ownership. When you own something, it becomes a part of you. You have to nurture it, care for it. Its well-being is tied to your own.

St. Cloud: That's a lot of its.

Arius: And out of the fear of loss, you find yourself obsessively protecting it. Having stuff is a full-time job.

St. Cloud: And where does the owning stuff end? It's ridiculous. How does one find the time for meaningful pursuits?

Arius: We wouldn't know about gravity if Newton was busy protecting his property.

St. Cloud: Can ya see Einstein putting shingles on the roof . . . there goes relativity.

Arius: Or Mozart working in the mines.

St. Cloud: Owning things is expensive as well. And to add insult to injury, it's all make believe.

Arius: A thief of time and resources. Exist only on paper.

St. Cloud: Like Albrecht said, "the only thing you own is the breath in your lungs, and even that not for long."

Arius: Now your quoting Albrecht?

St. Cloud: The man made a good point . . . and he don't smell so bad anymore.

Arius: (*circling clockwise*) Yada, yada, nada. We should approach this with some caution so as to not deprive ourselves of its benefits . . . while not being carried away by its burden. Albrecht can do whatever he pleases with his share. For our part, like you said, it's all make believe, but we'll play along and see what happens. What say you, St. Cloud?

St. Cloud: Mise en Scene![6] (*stirring the pot*) This is just about done. Time to call 'Close' back. . . . (*smiling*) I give you the honors.

Arius: If you like. (*stepping outside the campsite*) Ladies and . . . ah, her/he, . . . ah —

St Cloud: "Close"

Arius: Oh 'Close'. Dinner time . . . the turkey spaghetti is ready.

(*Albrecht and George return to the camp*)

George: How did that cook so fast?

Arius: Albrecht, I assume you have your own utensils?

Albrecht: Just like before. (*goes to the bush and retrieves two mess kits*) I have a stash in most of the camps in the country.

Arius: I'll bet you do.

George: We want for nothing wherever we go.
(*they each in turn serve themselves and take their seats*)

Albrecht: Now that I'm a partner, . . . I want a chair.

Arius: You have certainly come into your majority, Albrecht.

---

[6]Mise en scene: Set the stage

Albrecht: Well, I found my bracelet.

St. Cloud: He understood you!

Arius: It must be the food.

St. Cloud: Or part of Anthony became a part of him. They did spend a lot of time together.

George: (*speaking to Albrecht*) And what about me? Where am I gonna sit? I want a chair.

St. Cloud: You can sit in his lap for all I care.

Arius: (*authoritatively*) I'm afraid only partners have chairs.

Albrecht: (*pleading*) What can I do? Only partners have chairs. Look, you'll have this whole bench to yourself. Be patient. You can have my chair when we get married.

Arius: The shares are transferable, so —

George: Really?

Arius: Why not?

St. Cloud: I might consider selling my one third share.

Albrecht: (*talking with his mouth full*) George has big ideas about what we could do with this place.

Arius: Do tell us about George's big ideas.

St. Cloud: I'm all ears. (*they eat while talking*)

Albrecht: We figure we could give bed and board to other travelers as they pass through.

George: We could go into the hospitality business! Make a 'Travelers Inn'.

Arius: A 'Hobo Hilton'. That's interesting.

Albrecht: I could build lean-to's on the back half of the land. Like I learned back in survival training.

George: And I'll set up each lean-to with a fire pit, firewood and a teapot. Everything we need is right here. Plenty of wood for the lean-to's and the water tower is right down the track. Throw in gourmet cooking and we'll have travelers from all over the country banging on our door.

St. Cloud: Just what I've always wanted.

Arius: (*circling the pit clockwise holding his plate*) I could hold seminars, give lectures on things that matter. I would need a small amphitheater though, with ample seating.

George: Being the only game in town, we can charge whatever we want.

St. Cloud: Is that part of the intentional community bit?

George: (*annoyed, staring at Arius*) Why do you people walk in circles? It's like looking inside a watch. One going this way, the other that way, one going fast, the other slow.

Arius: It aids in the thinking process.

St. Cloud: Good for the digestion too. You should try it.

Arius: St. Cloud, you've been lamenting not having more time to spend perfecting you're cooking. For a while now.

St. Cloud: Yes I have.

Arius: Well, the gods of opportunity have entered your personal space.

St. Cloud: (*circling counter clockwise*) I have . . . they have. Let's see, . . . what would it take? I would need reliable suppliers. Suppliers capable of provisioning a varied menu. Apprentices, wait staff and seating in a relaxed atmosphere. Getting the music might be rough. But, worst-case scenario, I'll grab a couple of pickers from that Nashville crowd and give them a room and three squares a day.

Arius: And this might be as close as you'll get to a 'Dog and Pony' show. What say you, St. Cloud?

St. Cloud: I don't know . . . I'm not sure.

George: (*taking Albrecht's hand*) Come with me. I want to talk.

Albrecht: You can talk in front of them.

George: I don't want to talk with them, I wanna talk to you.

(*St. Cloud ignores them and continues.*)

St. Cloud: It's a lot of responsibility. More than with Anthony. Every morning I'd worry about how many workers were going to show up for work. Would the deliveries come before prep-time? Have the taxes been taken out of each day's tally? And why would I want to do so much work? . . . I don't have an answer to that yet.

Arius: Ah, good point. . . . I've always wanted an amphitheater, but the idea of managing maintenance crews, advertising people and disgruntled ticket holders is unbearable. Nothing could be worse than that. I too, have to consider this carefully.

(*There is silence as they pass each other, circling the firepit .*)

Arius: Still, I'm not quite ready to give up Anthony's gift without some kind of remuneration. Those who watch over us would deem it ungrateful were we to just walk away. Care should be taken. 'Measure twice, cut once" to use a cliché.

St. Cloud: Those were the days!

Arius: Yes, they were. But the 'now' demands we turn a profit. *(St. Cloud sits to listen, Arius continues in his circle)* Our friends over there have no money, as far as we know. I don't think Albrecht would part with his gold bracelet.

St. Cloud: I wouldn't take it. That would make bad Karma.

Arius: I agree. So how will we receive compensation for our holdings? How will we get paid?

St. Cloud: Perhaps, if we agreed to give away the proceeds, it might go more smoothly.

Arius: Yes, the law of Amra! That could work. It might increase our profits as well. Something to consider once we get the ball rolling.

St. Cloud: I've heard that before. *(circling counter clockwise, Arius sits.)* I think I know a way we can make it work for us. Hear me out. I will sell George my one third share, for one third of the one third share of the profits. To be picked up quarterly, paper money only, all currencies are welcome. Along with free meals and lodging of course. George will take ownership, assume all of the duties, responsibilities, and maintenance of the property.

Arius: Very clever St. Cloud. You make a profit, get away Scot-free and leave me with all the responsibility. Brilliant!

St. Cloud: One of us has to keep a stake or we'll have no claim. *(Sitting)* Ownership just ain't for me. The schedules, the bookkeeping, having to talk to people. It's not my cup of tea. You can't go nowhere cause people depend on you. And now I have to fear offending the guardians. When did that start? Why did this all happen?

Arius: Now, now, St. Cloud. Remember, this is an opportunity. (*stirring the pot*) Oh, here they come. Okay, St. Cloud, take it slow.

(*Albrecht and George enter the circle full of bravura. They sit on the bench, clasp their hands in their lap.*)

George: Gentlemen, before you start going round and round in circles, I, ah we, have a proposition to make. We would like to take St. Cloud up on his offer to sell his one third share in the property. I would like to purchase that share. At the moment I am low on capitol, but I am willing to sign a promissory note guaranteeing a portion of the profits from said share to be paid to the seller.

(*Arius and St Cloud smile at each other, pleased.*)

Arius: We'd have to be sure the plans are solid.

George: Solid as a rock. Our customers would arrive and depart when the train stops at the water tower.

Albrecht: Some would pick up a couple of beers and get back on the train, so we would have a retail business too. I'm in charge of that.

George: Lean-to's and campsites would be rented by the day or week.

St. Cloud: I would not be cooking or managing the restaurant, right?

George: Correct. We've agreed upon 'Whispering Willie' to be our chef.

Albrecht: He's the turnip king.

George: You may know him. He is famous for his 'Dumpster Stew Supreme'.

St. Cloud: I helped train him when he was a hobo apprentice.

George: Travelers, Mr. St. Cloud. Travelers!

St. Cloud: Well, we were hobos back then. And proud of it. Who asked you to change our name anyways?

Arius: People, let's stay focused. Politics is the ninth ring of Hell, and we have business to tend to.

George: It would have to be legal and registered with the State and County, otherwise, no go. Gentleman, if you stand aside and let us do our job, we might be able to make a go of this.

Arius: (*smiling*) Well, we'd have to go through Anthony, wouldn't you say St. Cloud, . . . but I'm sure he would be amenable.

St. Cloud: Of course, we're simpatico. (*to George*) He's an ASPY[7] you know . . . like we are.

Arius: All the best people are.

(*they pair off and talk amongst themselves*)

St. Cloud: I feel like this when I'm being surrounded by angry strangers.

Arius: Don't get all dramatic on me St. Cloud, things are going our way.

St. Cloud: We're making our own ball and chain . . . link by link.

Arius: This was your idea! One third of one third of one third. Your creation my friend.

---

[7] Asperger syndrome: Affecting the ability to socialize and communicate. A condition of the Autism spectrum, generally high functioning.

St. Cloud: Oh . . . that's right. . . . Just trying to be thorough … okay, never mind.

George: We've got to watch them. They're tricky. They're like spiders waiting for their web to shake. Let's be smart bugs. It could be painful.

Albrecht: Or worse, like taking a dump over a rattlesnake nest. By the way, where did you pick up all this law stuff from?

George: From Sid the liar. He was a lawyer before he became a traveler.

Albrecht: So what's that got to do with you?

George: We were close.

Albrecht: As 'close' as we are? —

Arius: (*taking center stage*) Fellow travelers and business partners, gather round. We have made our decision. We agree to the implementation of your vison to create a 'Hobo Hilton' at this location.

George: That's 'Travelers Hotel' Arius.

Arius: St. Cloud and I will leave 'tout suite' to consult and make arrangements with our benefactor for the transfer of title for a one third share of the enterprise. St. Cloud will sell George his one third share, for one third of the one third share of the profits. The proceeds will be picked up quarterly, paper money only with all currencies being welcome. Did I get that right St. Cloud?

St. Cloud: What he said--

Arius: The hotel will provide free meals and lodging of course. George will take ownership and assume all of the duties, responsibilities, and maintenance of the property.

Albrecht: 'All' of the responsibilities?

Arius: Well, . . . one third.

George: I want it in writing. And isn't it a conflict of interest for you as a partner to be negotiating for the seller? (*Albrecht smiles proudly.*)

Arius: No more than Albrecht looking out for your interest.

St. Cloud: Besides, we don't have anything to write with.

(*George goes to the bush and brings back legal pad and pen*)

George: Here ya go, green tie.

Albrecht: (*approvingly*) Sid the liar taught you well.

St. Cloud: Sid the Liar! . . . I should have known.

Arius: Ah . . . of course.

St. Cloud: Whatever happened to the 'Hobo code of Honor'?

George: It's been replaced with something better. A forgettable part of our history that's time has come.

St. Cloud: Writing things down is what made this world so crazy.

George: Tell it to the judge!

(*St. Cloud begins to write down the proposal.*)

Arius: (*whispering to St. Cloud*) This is beginning to look like a scene from 'The Treasure of Sierra Madre'.

St. Cloud: It is. Just a different place and time. The stage is the same. Let's just get this done and be on our way.

(*St. Cloud finishes and hands the legal pad to George.*)

Arius: And with that, Albrecht, George, we will prepare for our journey.

(Albrecht and George dance, congratulating each other)

George: And you defended me. My knight to the rescue.

Albrecht: Nothing's too good for my 'close.'

St. Cloud: I think we should walk backwards. It will help us regroup.

Arius: I suspect you're right. It would be reassuring.

(they shoulder their belongings and walk backwards. They all patronize each other, speaking disingenuously.)

Arius: Well, we'll be on our way. Next stop is Anthony's place to get the paperwork signed.

George: Great! Hurry back, we'll be waiting!

Albrecht: Arius, can we use your amphitheater for our overflow guests?

Arius: Certainly, certainly . . . whatever will make the business grow! Now, we must go.

St. Cloud: We're going to have to turn around before we reach the tunnel you know.

Arius: Of course . . . together . . . one, two, three.

George: We did it. They bought the whole spiel!

Albrecht: You played them perfectly.

Arius: Brilliant! They fell right into our hands.

St. Cloud: And gave us everything we wanted.

(Entering the tunnel, their voices echo from within)

Arius: Now, where were we?

St. Cloud: Sciamachy, and before that, Clichés.

Arius: Ah yes, burritos that encompass almost everything.

Curtain

Pettakere

A One Act Play

Time: Thirty-nine thousand years ago
Place: An island in the Indonesian archipelago
Characters:

Aliran: A tall, boney young man with shoulder-length hair. He is wearing a loin-cloth and carries a woven satchel. He is known in the village for seeing things that are not there and for talking about things no one has heard of. Willful, with a penetrating gaze, he is looked upon with caution.

Suma: A wispy young girl with hair to her waist. She is pretty and of marriageable age. She wears a loose-fitting dress, tied at the shoulders. She knows little about how the world works and is there because of her love for Aliran.

Big Nose: Suma's father

Shaman: Tall, thin with long grey hair and white beard.
People of the village.

Scene One

Painted on the walls of a cave on the island of Sulawesi are some of the oldest works of art created by man. The curtain opens to a grove lit by a full moon. Center stage is a pathway carved into a hillside. It leads to a cave above, which is sacred to the people of the area. The forest surrounding the grotto is pitch black and we find Aliran and Suma entering stage left, holding hands. They stop to rest at the bottom of the path that leads to the cave.

Suma: (*sitting on a log*) I need to rest and eat something.

Aliran: (*sits on a rock, opening his satchel*) I brought some food for us. We have bananas, mangos, and candle nuts —

Suma: Mmm . . . gimme, gimme. (*She eats voraciously*) Why did we have to come here so early? Even the birds are still asleep.

Aliran: Because it's quiet at this time and the gods will hear us better.

Suma: How do you know this?

Aliran: (*popping candle nuts as he speaks*) I can only say I feel it in my body and know it to be true. My body says the rising Sun will push our message to the heavens, beyond the stars, to the huts of the Great Ones.

Suma: Do the Great Ones live in huts?

Aliran: Yes they do. In huts as big as volcanos. They made their huts of eucalyptus trees, and like the bark of the eucalyptus, they are the colors of a rainbow.

Suma: Is that what the Shamans say?

Aliran: I never asked them. It's knowledge come from the Ancients.

Suma: But already the Shamans speak to the gods for the people. Why do we have to speak with them?

Aliran: We don't need other people to speak to the heavens for us. We can do it ourselves.

Suma: But what will I say to them? They don't know me!

Aliran: You can tell them we have joined our spirits, and we wish to be together, forever.

Suma: But the Elders have said I must be with the first son of the Anoa tribe.

Aliran: And WE say, we must be together.

Suma: But we will be shamed and chased from the village if we don't do as the elders tell us. We will die in the wilderness without our people.

Aliran: We will not be shamed, and we will not die. Let us see what the heavens say. If they say to follow the Elders, I will follow. Until then I will listen to what I know to be true.

Suma: More mango . . . gimme.

Aliran: *(handing her the fruit)* Our hearts beat together Suma. The gods will see that and smile upon us. I have brought bright colors to get their attention. They cannot ignore us.

Suma: Aliran, *(worried)* where did you get the magic powder?

Aliran: I helped the Shaman make his powder and made some for us too. We crushed rocks and squeezed plant juice onto it, using different rocks to make the different colors. Look, *(reaching into his bag)* this rock makes red, and this one makes yellow. We took burned bones from the fire pit and mixed them with the fat of a pig to make it thick. Our spit will make it one. It is wonderful knowledge, Suma. Someday, when my knowledge is complete, I will share it with the people of the village.

Suma: *(squinting)* Doesn't sound good tasting.

Aliran: Think of the taste of our love forever.

Suma: Yes! *(with a big smile)* How could that taste bad? . . . it will taste like flower water.

Aliran: Just like you. *(Handing her a banana, biting into a mango)* The gods have already smiled upon us.

Suma: I just hope they listen. I don't want to leave you to live on another Island. A toothless old woman in the village told me there are often bad winds that circle the Anoa peoples' island. And she says the sharks feed there. Her grandmother married into the Anoa people and one time when she was going home to visit her mother, the sharks ate her. She never made it back to our village.

Aliran: I have heard the same. The fishermen tell me the Orca hunt in pacts and have destroyed whole fishing crews, playing with them like trinkets . . . gone in just a few minutes.

Suma: I hope the heavens are listening today.

Aliran: Don't worry, my colors are very loud. We will be heard on the farthest star. I have it all planned out and soon, with their permission, I will build us a hut by the waterfall. *(He rises and stretches)* The air is warming. We should go. *(He takes her hand to help her onto the pathway.)*

Suma: Will the Heavens understand?

Aliran: Let us go and find out.

The Curtain Falls as they make their way up the path.

Scene Two

The curtain rises to Aliran and Suma standing at the cave opening, holding hands, staring into the hollowed-out chamber. The first light of the day shines behind them and dimly illuminates the interior. Above, a break in the rock formation forms an oculus, which casts a beam of light into the cave. Stone benches, semi-circular, enclose a fire pit facing one of the cave walls.

Aliran: Come this way Suma. _(He puts his arm around her shoulder and they walk slowly down to center stage)_

Suma: I'm scared Aliran. It's cold here, and dark.

Aliran: It will warm soon, when the sun rises. We will be able to see better too. Come, it's not far. This way.

Suma: How do we know there are no animals here? They could eat us!

Aliran: The Shaman says the animals on the walls keep the walking animals away. I've never seen animals here, so it must be true.

Suma: Have you been here before?

Aliran: Many times, with the Shaman and the Elders. Sometimes I come by myself, when the moon is full, to see the pictures in my head. The moonlight fills the cave and makes everything clear. (*He leads her to the stone benches behind the fire pit*) Come, here is where we sit to study the wall. (*Aliran digs through his satchel and removes a conch shell containing the paint, a brush made of leaves, and a coconut holding water*)

Suma: Look, (*pointing*) there are stars on that wall, just like in the heavens. And someone has marked it with their hand.

Aliran: As we will. The Ancients put the stars there in a time before our people can remember. What is above, is below the Ancients' say. All that we see and touch are but reflections of the light from the heavens. The stars are the islands of the great waters of the sky, just like the islands on which we live and fish. It is like when you see your face, in a pool of still water, looking back at you. What is above is below. When we make our hands on the wall, they will become canoes that will travel from star to star, carrying our message to the home of the gods. (*Aliran stands, holding the conch shell*) The sun is rising so we must continue. Let me show you what we will do. This is the way of the Ancients, as passed down from long ago. We will take a finger of paint from the conch and put it in our mouths. Then a sip of water from the coconut and mix it around. We place our hand on the wall and spit the color all around the hand. Be sure to get between the fingers. The paint on our hand, we will sweep away with this (*holding the brush for her to see*) and that will make the colors very strong, all around our marker. Your hand will be red for one or two days so--

Suma: Then everyone will know I've been here.

Aliran: All the women of the village will be jealous. (*They walk together to the cave wall*) Come, you first.

Suma: Why do I have to go first?

Aliran: Because you're prettier, and the gods like pretty girls. Put your hand on the wall below the other one. Spread your fingers wide and press hard. Suma, as I spit the paint around your hand, send the pictures in your mind to your hand and wish them to be so. Make your wish with your whole body so the gods will hear you, loud and clear.

(Aliran scoops a finger full of paint from the conch and a sip of water and mixes them together in his mouth. He spits the paint around her hand, working the color into the rock with the brush)

Aliran: Now you. *(Suma takes a finger full of paint and a sip of water and mixes them in her mouth with a grimace)*

Aliran: *(laughing)* If it tasted good you would eat it instead of painting the hand. *(Suma leaning into the wall spits the paint around her hand. Aliran works the paint into the rock with the brush.)*

Tell the gods what you wish for Suma, tell them with all your heart. (Aliran steps back to view the wall) Come, see what we have done.

Suma: *(stepping back, she gasps)* Is that my hand? It's so beautiful!

Aliran: Yes, it is. Now I must place my hand beside yours so they will travel together. Come, stand beside me, hold these things. *(He hands Suma the conch shell and the coconut. He takes a finger full of paint and a sip of water and goes to the wall. He spits the paint on the wall, outlining his hand, working it into the rock with the brush.)* It will need more. Now you. *(Suma fills her mouth with paint and water and spits it around Aliran's hand as he works the brush. There is the rumble of thunder in the distance.)* It is done! We have made our message to the gods.

(Aliran takes the coconut and rinses his mouth with the water and spits it into the fire pit. He hands it to Suma for her to do the same. He takes her hand and they return to the stone bench to view the wall.)

Suma: Look, our hands are reaching for each other.

Aliran: They will join together in the sky. *(The stage dims.)*

Suma: It has grown dark!

Aliran: Rain clouds must be covering the sun. They will pass.

(With a loud burst of thunder, they hold each other. Lightning flashes, creating a strobe light. The cave trembles and the couple whimper in fear.)

Suma: The gods are angry with us. What can we do?

Aliran: We must wait to see what they say.

(With another burst of lightning the daylight returns. A beam of light pours through the oculus forming a spotlight which shines upon the hands on the wall, making them glow.)

Suma: Aliran, look our hands are so bright. What does it mean?

Aliran: It means the gods have heard our message . . . Now, we wait for their decision, we must close our eyes and listen.

(Villagers have gathered at the entrance of the cave. The Shaman and Big Nose stand in front of the group peering into the cave apprehensively.)

Shaman: Aliran! . . . I thought so. What have you done?

Big Nose: Daughter, is that you? Why is your face red? What has happened to your hand? Is that blood?

(Shaman steps into the cave cautiously, following the beam of light from the oculus to the wall)

Shaman: Your daughter is fine, Big Nose. That is the magic paint that you see. It is used to send messages to the gods. Aliran, what have you said to the gods?

Aliran: We have asked to be together, as one.

Shaman: The crocodiles have lined the shore, facing the village. The men cannot reach their canoes to fish. The warty pigs have surrounded our huts making terrible sounds. The lightning and thunder have frightened the women and children. Have you asked the gods to do this?

Aliran: No, we did not ask the gods to do these things. We asked for their permission to join together, and now we wait for their answer.

Shaman: Your answer has come. It is clear the gods have favored your request and are letting the people know they want us to honor this request.

Big Nose: But Suma is promised to the first son of the Anoa people. We have exchanged gifts. It is soon to take place.

Shaman: You have many daughters, Big Nose. You can give the Anoa people another daughter. The first son of their tribe already has many wives. It will make little difference to him. It is the bond between the tribes that matter, and they too will not want to offend the gods.

Big Nose: It is not the way of our people to break an agreement. We must be true to the words we speak.

Shaman: You will not break the agreement. You will be true to your words. You have offered your daughter in marriage, in peace and friendship, and so you shall do that. Just a different daughter. I will speak with the Elders of the Anoa people. They will also want the men to return to fish the waters and the women to harvest the fruits of the land, just as we do. If you follow my words it will be so. For all the people.

Big Nose: (*glaring at Aliran and Suma*) I will agree to what you say if it is acceptable to the Elders of the Anoa.

Shaman: We do not have a choice. The gods have spoken and we must follow their wishes. (*Shaman walks over to Aliran and Suma who are still transfixed by the images on the wall.*) Aliran, the Heavens have heard your request and granted your wish. You have learned well and made powerful magic. The gods have shown the people who will succeed me in the future. Go now, it is time for you to make ready for a joining ceremony.

(*Aliran gathers the paint, the brush and the coconut into his woven basket. He takes Suma's hand and they make their way to the cave opening. The people stand aside to allow them to pass, gazing with wonder upon the couple who have petitioned the gods and changed their future.*)

The Curtain Falls

Cirey

Act I
Scene One

(Curtain rises, chorus descends horse shoe stairway. Chorister's mill about below, exchanging greetings and gossip. Chorus sings.)

"What Have You Heard"

What have you heard?
what have you heard?
in Paris and Fontainebleau
what have you heard?
Tell me, tell me! don't tantalize me,
who is in favor at Versailles.
What have you heard?
what have you heard?
no matter how stupid
inane or absurd.
Tell us, tell us,
something that's scandalous,
who has been exiled and why?

(Prince De Croy and Mme De Graffigny step out of the crowd, center stage)

<u>*Prince De Croy*</u>*: I'll give you a little morsel*
that I have heard rumored,
now Pompadour is ruling the nest.
She's been busy decorating,
goes about dictating,
just how things should run
here in France.
And young Fredrick of Prussia
has assumed the throne.
 He has promised changes
throughout his realm.
There are no ladies attending his court,
only poets and dancers, flatterers all."

<u>*Mme De Graffigny:*</u>

There is a certain young lady of Nobel high birth,
has a dozen or so lovers who wait at her door.
There's a duel taking place right now as we speak,
as she dances the Gigue with abandon and glee.
There are no new exiles, though a famous one returns! Voltaire, the
playwright, will make Paris his home. He will be here this evening
with the Duc Richelieu, so watch yourselves ladies should they fancy
you.

Chorus
> *What have you heard?*
> *what have you heard?*
> *don't bore us with trifles,*
> *Just give us the dirt.*
> *Tell us, tells us,*
> *something that's scandalous,*
> *Who has been exiled and why?*

(The crowd notices Voltaire, Emilie and Richelieu entering the party.
They rush to greet Voltaire, singing)

Voltaire's Waltz

Francois Marie Arouet
the one they call Voltaire.
A most darling little man
who whenever he can
upsets the institutions of France.
Francois Marie Arouet
the toast of all Paris.
Add some charm to his wit,
with a theatrical twist,
and Viola! The playwright Voltaire!
He has quartered at the Bastille,
was exiled, became an Anglophile.

Came back to Paris with strange idea's.
With friends in high places,
some clever business deals,
made our Francois a wealthy man.
François Marie Arouet
a favored philosophie.

<u>Ladies:</u> *With his magical ideas*
he will charm you my dear,

<u>Men</u>: *and buy up your debt, (ha, ha,ha)*
with a good bit of cheer!
Francois Marie Arouet
the one they call Voltaire.
When the Duc Richelieu
has had his way with you,
(ha, ha, ha) enter the playwright Voltaire.
He has quartered at the Bastille,
was exiled, became an Anglophile.
Came back to Paris with strange ideas.
With friends in high places,
some clever business deals,
made our Francois a wealthy man.

(Voltaire breaks away from the crowd and walks down stage to the footlights and addresses the live audience)

<u>Voltaire:</u> "They never get it right. Good evening, I am Francois Marie Arouet; the one they call Voltaire. I apologize for interrupting this evening's musicale but I felt I should do away with some of the rumors and innuendos surrounding these wonderful characters. We will show you actual scenes from the lives of real people. The gossip, the babbling of the herd, is the substance with which our friends here fill their lives. Accuracy has never been a requirement. Some of it has even been called

history. Very little is faithful. This will be a slice of a most delightful morsel in history. Everything seemed possible. The sage Isaac Newton gave us a system with which to order the entire world. Men of daring were changing the economic order; questioning the very veracity of our paradigms on man and God and law. Those with imagination were creating themselves, thriving in the new understanding of the individual and society. Here is our part in that panorama. Together with my muse, my partner, my companion, my lover (*gesturing towards Emilie*)_we set out to make our own little contribution, and that is the story of Cirey! A magical place where one need only bring their ideas, their passion, their insights into the miracles of this wondrous creation, to gain entrance. But why only speak of it ? Come…join us…we will show you. We will take you to Cirey!

(*A reprise of Voltaire's waltz is played. Voltaire and Richelieu meet center stage.*)

Richelieu: Ah! The ladies are especially beautiful this evening Francois. And they appear most willing —

(*Having different conversations*)

Voltaire: It is good to be back in Paris —

Richelieu: Is there anyone in particular you have your eye on?

Voltaire: though nothing has changed —

Richelieu: I don't want to be running into you in some dark corridor in the middle of the night … yet again!

Voltaire: it's as though I have walked into the same conversation without interruption —

Richelieu: you're not listening! (*annoyed*)

Voltaire: Sorry, … what were you saying?

Richelieu: Which one of these lovely beauties excites your fancy?

Voltaire: There is only one woman.

Richelieu: Ha! You have forgotten how to count.

Voltaire: Emilie! Why on earth would I want a coiffured mannequin when I could have a woman of intellect?

Richelieu: We will see how long that lasts —

Voltaire: And sumptuous as well.

Richelieu: (*greeting a lady of court*) Mademoiselle…..Mon plaisir (*turning to Voltaire*) Methinks too much of the dour demeanor of the English has rubbed off on my friend the satyr. (*eyeing a courtier*) Now that's an interesting prospect. …. A bien tot! (*Richelieu slides up to his prey*)

Voltaire: See you later

(*A reprise of Voltaire's waltz as Voltaire mills about the room. Prince.DeCroy and Mme. De Graffigny, from opposite sides of the stage meet center stage to the bass line of what have you heard.*)

Mme De Graffigny: It seems the Count D'Argent cannot keep his hands to himself.

Prince De Croy: The countess is away, taking the waters at Plombier. . . .and, when the cats away —

Mme De Graffigny: Would you look at Madame Celi'….she can barely move she's bound so tight, . . . if that hair piece were any taller she would fall over.

(*a servant with towels rushes to madam Celi*)

Prince De Croy: It appears she also has a week bladder ... Celi' in a puddle.

Mme De Graffigny: *(laughing)* And she can't move. *(peering over her fan)* I see the Marquise Du Chatelet has added the playwright to her list of mathematicians and academics . . . I wonder what made His majesty change his mind and allow his return?

Prince De Croy: Mademoiselle E'toile is an admirer. She has convinced His majesty that Voltaire is a national treasure. She has brought Rameau under her wing as well and has assembled quite a little theatrical troupe.

Mme De Graffigny: with E'toile center stage I am sure.

Prince De Croy: She has become Voltaire's champion at court.

Mme De Graffigny: Along with Richelieu and Chatelet and on and on and on.

Prince De Croy: Just goes to show that with enough money to buy friends, even a bourgeois can 'strut his stuff.'

(There is a commotion and much chatter at the card tables. Emilie appears to be bewildered. Voltaire, who has been weaving his way through the crowd, rests his hand on her shoulder.)

Voltaire: Emilie?

Emilie: *(turning to Voltaire)* My system isn't working ... not even close . . . something is wrong.

Voltaire: You are just refining your method. It will come.

Emilie: Numbers always speak the truth, they never lie.

Voltaire: But systems and equations, they are like musical instruments. They need to be tuned, to create their harmonies.

They have to be liberated *(turning to a couple of courtiers who are listening with rapt attention)* so they can fall into their natural order. *(He leads the small group away from the tables and continues)* During my travels I would enjoy late night suppers with Bolingbrooke discussing these very matters.

Lady 1: Bahlinboo *(trying to pronounce the English scientist's name with difficulty)*

Lady2: Baalingbok, Bawlnbuk *(they both giggle)*

Gentleman: The English have twisted their language into unspeakable knots. Why don't they just speak French...I can't understand a word they say.

(There is another commotion at the top of the stairs. Adrienne Lecouvreur the famous Opera singer has entered with her entourage. All the while Emilie has been absorbed in her card game. Her demeanor is showing her frustration at her losses. Voltaire notices and returns to her side.)

Emilie: Francois, nothing is working. I have lost heavily; borrowed twice and cannot recoup my monies.

Voltaire: How much have you lost?

Emilie: Almost a million.

Voltaire: Mon Dieu woman! What have you done? *(whispering in her ear)* How are you ever going to pay back this money?

Emilie: Don't distract me.

Voltaire: This is madness

Emilie: Francois! please, I have to concentrate

Voltaire: How could you expect to win when you are playing with a gaggle of cheats.

(A player at the table has overheard Voltaire and begins to whisper to those around him Emilie notices the growing commotion.)

Emilie: Now you've done it! Pretend nothing has happened. Act normal.

Voltaire: Normal! moi !

(Prince De Croy and Mme De Graffigny pick up the news and go out into the crowd to spread the word. The drum roll from "whut have you heard" plays as the murmuring of the crowd grows louder. Richelieu sees what is going on; a courtier whispers in his ear.)

Richelieu: Voltaire! . . . not again!

(He works his way to Voltaire and Emilie)

Richelieu: We must leave. *(emphatically)*

Emilie: But I have just started to win back my —

Richelieu: Now!!

Voltaire: Walk this way *(Ala Mel Brooks)*

Richelieu: No! this way, up the stairs….don't look at anyone, no eye contact, just head for the door.

(A reprise of Voltaire's waltz played flat, drum roll from what have you heard plays.)

Curtain

Scene two

(The curtain rises to a country scene outside of Paris. It is late in the night. The carriage is propped up, leaning to its side, missing one wheel. Emilie is pacing, arms folded, agitated. Voltaire is sitting on a log, staring into a fire, poking it with a stick. Voltaire's valet, Longchamp, wheel in hand is seen talking to the coachman downstage. He informs Emilie and Voltaire of their situation.)

<u>Longchamp:</u> The coachman tells me there is a village two miles down the road. There is lodging and a blacksmith there. I will arrange for the repair and have food heated for you at the inn. It will take a couple of hours to get transport to the village though. I should be off to see to the arrangements.

<u>Voltaire:</u> Thank you Longchamp

<u>Emilie:</u> Thank you Longchamp.

(They both sit silent and sullen. Their tension weighs heavily on the smoke of the dying embers. Emilie leaps to her feet, wrapping her blanket around her shoulders, pacing, quite agitated.)

<u>Emilie:</u> How could you! What were you thinking? Is there some kind of obscene pleasure you get from upsetting and alienating people.

<u>Voltaire:</u> I didn't think anyone would understand what I was saying.

<u>Emilie:</u> I had to leave with big losses … what! Understand! Do you think we are only people who speak English! True, most of them can't dress themselves, but in that same group are ambassadors, poets, statesmen! All of whom speak English and German, Italian! What were you thinking.

Voltaire: Perhaps thoughtless, but I was right in what I said.

Emilie: It doesn't even matter whether you are right or not. It was the Queens card party and such things never happen at the Queens card party, even if they do! It is the "Way" we live. It is in our blood.

Voltaire: You may have the same blood in your veins as that inbreed clique Emilie, but yours, it's pulse is wild and searching, harmonizing to a higher sphere.

Emilie: Don't start rhapsodizing, it won't work.

Voltaire: (*hands behind his back pacing and grinning*) I seem to recall a young Marquise, getting into the wrong carriage at one of the Queens outings and her endless complaints about being silently ostracized for months for the faux pas. A violation of decorum, I believe it was called.

Emilie: And it took me months to right that one. An unfortunate incident! Hardly the same thing.

Voltaire: But it is the same thing! That world is a puppet show. A puppet show where the players are human and are directed by the same puppeteers; pulling the same strings according to the same script. And where there is no drama they will invent one, reinvent one, over and over again. That is the "Way" they are.

Emilie: Go back to the rhapsodizing!

Voltaire: (*still pacing, absorbed in thought*) There must be another way.

Emilie: It does sound silly—

Voltaire: I mean these people are ridiculous. You suggest something new, just an idea, and they claim that your destroying the very foundation of their society. Heaven forbid you should question their 'Divine Right' to treat us like chattel and harvest the fruits of our labor.

Emilie: *(to herself)* There must be another way . . . the court is a rather empty and boring farce. I would much rather work on this new mathematics' . . . And I must understand this Newton and there is the children's education to consider.

Voltaire: Staying in Paris is like living in a Lion's den —

Emilie: It's so hard to concentrate with all the distractions at court —

Voltaire: Whenever they decide to use their arrest warrants, I'm right there to be had. Back to the Bastille and bribing guards.

Emilie: The Marquis is always away at his post and our estate is in order, . . . other than this monstrous debit.

Voltaire: I have to find a way around this. Somehow, we have to turn this situation to our advantage. What is it we have working for us? What do we need? How do we avoid backward people who happen to have power? Between the two of us, we certainly have enough resources to shape events to our advantage. What is it we need to do? What do I need? . . . Emilie, if you could have things exactly your way, just as you would like them, what would it look like? What is it that you would need?

Emilie: I would have to have a place to study. Away from the distractions of court; where the children could play in the fresh air and I could ride my horses. I would like to have among my friends people who are thinking about things that matter; who are working on great ideas. I would like to live free as a man, yet feel and experience life as a woman. I would choose to live on Olympus! And Francois! I have had this wonderful dream. I want to translate Newton into French so that all the people of France can read and understand his wonderful ideas.

Voltaire: I have the history of Louis IV to finish . . . and the last edit of my English Letters. The Theatre Franchise has asked me for another play. I have been dying to do some scientific experiments of my own. Jump right into it. I could do my experiments the same way Gravesande does with measuring and weighing and observation. Why can I not become Voltaire the scientist as well?

Emilie: "The best of all possible worlds"

Voltaire: Now's not the time for that, Emilie. What do we need?… A place. A place to do all these things . . . away from court and for me, away from the police. A place where we can serve up our dinners and entertainments. Emilie, (*pacing, rubbing his hands together, blowing on them*) on one of our trips we stopped at a small chateau in the country.

Emilie: Yes, Cirey. A family home of the Chatelet. Why, what are you thinking?

Voltaire: It would be perfect!

Emilie: It's in terrible condition, we could never live there!

Voltaire: A few repairs—

Emilie: Ah! A few repairs! (*pacing again*) … And it's two days away from Paris.

Voltaire: And close to the border. (*smiling*)

Emilie: My husband would never accept it.

Voltaire: Of course he will! I will supply all the money necessary for the repairs and its upkeep in exchange for living there. I have enough money from my business ventures to do whatever we want. (*bowing*) Thank you Jean Law! The upgraded property is his, so when I walk away, he is left with a restored Chateau. It is a winning combination for all.

Emilie: There will be talk. The last thing we need now is more talk.

Voltaire: There will always be talk, no matter what we do. Better to give them something to talk about rather than leaving it to their imaginations.

(Emilie, staring off, sways as she sings the name Cirey. The orchestra begins the music of CIREY. Voltaire, hands behind his back, pacing, begins the song).

Chanson de Cirey

Voltaire: We'll need a great library

Emilie: Cirey

Voltaire: The most up to date laboratory

Emilie: Cirey

Voltaire: A theater for our music and plays

Emilie: Cirey

Voltaire: Come on Emilie, what do you say?

Emilie: We'll start a whole new life,

Voltaire: Cirey

*Emilie: Away from Paris, Fontainebleau and Versailles.
We will set a fine table and invite all our friends,*

a house filled with theater, music and dance.

Voltaire: Unfold the mysteries of the universe.

Emilie: Clothe our love, in numbers and in verse.

Voltaire: Expose superstition, study the stars.

Emilie: Read Leibnitz, Newton, Galileo, Descartes.

Voltaire: The work will take some time. We'll design it ourselves and make it sublime.

Emilie: Cirey

Voltaire: We will start with our quarters, add rooms for the guest. With bathtubs and privies, only the best!

Together: We will become, the "Hotel Du Monde,"
for the latest and the greatest minds in the world!
We'll build a Temple to the future of mankind,
where all understand the wonders of creation, the dignity of man.
We will set a fine table and invite all our friends!
With music and poetry, science and math.
Cirey!

(The song progresses to a dance number. A scrim depicting Cirey drops slowly during the dance. Workmen carrying ladders and various tools begin to people the stage. The song ends in a rousing tutti as the scrim depicting Cirey becomes more clear.)

End of Act One

Act II

Scene One

(The curtain opens to a large salon. The construction work has not been finished. There is a scaffold set up in an alcove and various workman's tools are strewn about the room, creating obstacles. Center is a table with blueprints, a rule and compass, etc. The theme Cirey plays in the background and there are maids carrying laundry, men with arms full of firewood, a cook passing through with a goose dangling from his hand. They have to navigate their way around the tools and each other. Emilie and Maupertuis enter. Emilie is carrying a roll of blueprints and looks as though she has been hands on in the work going on throughout the house. She tosses the blueprints on the table.)

Emilie: I spend my days with carpenters and masons. It is endless! You have no idea how thick the workers can be. Some of them don't know the difference between a window and a door. Their supervisors need supervision! I tell them what I want, then come back later and find they have built something entirely different. It's exhausting!

Maurpertuis: And you have been neglecting your studies.(*shaking his finger at her disapprovingly*)

Emilie: That reminds me, I have to arrange for the children's tutor. (*looking through the papers on the table*) I have a list of candidates somewhere around here, though Voltaire is pressing me to hire some misfit devotee of his. And you are right, I have been neglecting my mathematics. As soon as this madness is under control, we will have to double down and catch up. (*A notary comes in and presents Emilie with papers to sign. She does so hurriedly and dismisses him*)

Maupertuis: Emilie, why do you bother. Why even concern yourself with these matters. It is best left to your husband to oversee these things. It is beneath you, Emilie.

Emilie: The management of one's life is certainly not beneath them! Do you mean to suggest that my time would be better spent laboring for hours over my appearance, just so that I can gossip with the ladies or flatter rotund magistrates? Petitions on family matters are one thing, and I gladly accept the responsibility, but whole years can pass in these types of doldrums. It is a boring somnambulism, to say the least.

Maupertuis: Emilie, you are in the middle of nowhere! Are you to waste your privilege out here in the woods? And what of our lessons?

Emilie: You can join us here, where we will create a world governed by intellect. With our imaginations we create the world, Mon cher.

Maupertuis: (*pedantically*) Emilie your mother has asked me to speak with you to convey the wish that you return to your duties and responsibilities, and maintain the family's position at court which your father worked so hard to establish. She feels you may hold my opinion in some regard and will listen to reason. Many others have expressed concern over this self-imposed exile you have chosen. Most courtiers live in dread of being exiled and here you seem to prefer this self-flagellation to the pleasures of court.

Emilie: Flagellation? More like exaltation! . . . If you equate exploring this clockwork universe with the most intelligent man I have ever known with flagellation, I am at a loss to explain.

Maupertuis: His exile does not have to be your own. His letters from England have already created a stir and he knows well what the outcome will be.

Emilie: Monsieur, were I Florent-Claude or one of your good fellows you would be lauding me for my efforts! "Grand fellow, a man of daring" (*waving her arms in a grand gesture*). But because I am a woman, you suppose that your understanding, your "superior" male intellect, which has left the world in the chaos of war and suffering, knows what is best for me. It is only because I am a woman that you question my decisions.

(*A maid approaches Emilie with an armful of curtain material. She flips through several swathes, choosing one, and dismisses her*).

Emilie: Monsieur! With all do respect, I very much disagree!
  (Emilie is livid. She starts the song 'If I wore a man's clothes')

'If I Wore a Man's Clothes'

If I wore a man's clothes,
You would not be here, critiquing my decisions.
If I wore a man's clothes,
You would never dare, to question my erudition.
Or any of my ambitions,
with your feeble suppositions.
If I wore a man's clothes,
you would laugh at my brazen adventure!
Cheer me on, glass raised, praising my daring.
If I wore a man's clothes!

Maupertuis: Emilie, I am ashamed to say you are correct. I should know better. It is just as you say and obviously, I am a part of it.

(Emilie runs to hug Maupertuis)

Emilie: Mon Cher, I would love so much to have your support and your approval. You could help. You could help explain to Paris that this will be a place where reason and intellect reign. Away from the constraints of the church and the state and the babbling herd. There are many who hold you in great esteem and you could carry our message to the salons and the Academe.

Maupertuis: They are not used to women being brilliant. Crafty and designing, yes; a woman of superior intellect is something they are not accustomed to.

Emilie: They only have to look beyond the borders of France to see there is a new world evolving and women are a part of it. Look to Italy.

Maupertuis: Yes, I admit we are rather constrained and provincial in our attitudes.

(Voltaire and Richelieu enter the room. Voltaire has blueprints in his hand. They are in the middle of a conversation.)

Richelieu: Mon Ami, come back to Paris, I will clear up all the misunderstandings.

(Voltaire catches sight of Emilie and Maupertuis and loudly changes the subject)

Voltaire: You must send my regards to Mme E'toile congratulating her on her new coat of arms.

Richelieu: (*Catching on*) Yes, yes for sure.

(Emilie not wanting Voltaire and Richelieu to be privy to her conversation, gestures Maupertuis to follow her)

Emilie: And the dining room is nearly finished. *(leaving the room)*

(Relaxing, Voltaire and Richelieu continue their conversation.)

Voltaire: There is something that needs watching with that fellow. I'm sorry, I didn't want Emilie to overhear what we were saying. She's been getting in the way of everything lately. Where I put windows, she puts doors; She's changing staircases into chimneys and chimneys into staircases. *(looking through the papers on the desk)* What were you saying?

Richelieu: You must have no idea how difficult you are making things! The Marquis is stationed with me; he is a friend.

Someone whom I depend on the battlefield, as well as at court. A reasonable man, but proud as well!

Voltaire: Then you can reason with him. Show him how this whole project is to his advantage. Present it to him as a brilliant business decision on his part. The care and maintenance of his ancestral home at no cost to himself.

Richelieu: And the rumors and innuendo?

Voltaire : Emilie has her own wing, the house will always have guests. The semblance of propriety is all in place. Florent-Claude is also a friend of mine and as far as he is concerned, I am but an amusement, a new fancy for an inquisitive wife. Makes him rather fashionable, wouldn't you say?

Richelieu: I would rather say that you are crazy. I would say that together we have become the toasts of Paris. There is not a single salon that does not beg our attendance. I would say that we live a charmed life and we should enjoy it while we can. Death is for certain, disease is common. The cold is real, and the future is fluid. It could all end tomorrow, on the battlefield or on the way to the opera. I would say the point of this life is to embrace our good fortune, not to constantly test it.

Voltaire: I do see your reasoning. And it is all very tempting, I must admit.

Richelieu: And rewarding. Good God man, you have an apartment at the Palace of Versailles.

Voltaire: Right above the toilet.

Richelieu: Even right above the toilet, you are there, right at the center of the world.

Voltaire: The smell is abominable.

(The music to 'Richelieu's waltz' begins softly in the orchestra.)

<u>Richelieu:</u> It's tolerable

<u>Voltaire:</u> Easy for you to say, your apartment is right next to the King's mistress. *(Richelieu begins his song.)*

'Richelieu's Waltz'

Why? All this questioning "Why"
Each one believing,
that "this one goes that way," and "that one goes this way"
But why? The eternal why!
Why, champion these crazy ideas,
when the ladies are waiting.
How can I believe in things I can't see?
That hold me to earth, this supposed gravity.
Ideas so fantastic
sometimes I fear for your sanity!
Le bon heur
All the world is our stage
and were stunning.
All the members at court
think you clever and smart,
Et "Je suis le gran militaire"
Le Bon vie
Our life is a banquet
why through it away!
Why bring sand to the beach
or chase dreams out of reach,
When our table is sumptuous and full.
Why, this incessant questioning "Why"
What does it get you?

Maupertuis is running off to the pole, while you're in the forest burning coal,
The Marquise sings numbers as though they were poetry and verse.
It's a Curse!

Le Bon temp
In this wonderful age that we're living.
Rich in beauty and grace,
ah! the sumptuous Palais,
where gardens run clear to the sky.
Mon ami,
Come back to Paris
We're such a great team.
You can charm with your verse,
and I with my girth,
we're at the top of our game.
Why, create all these problems
Why! can't you go with the flow.
Galileo and Newton, Leibnitz, Descartes,
have all worked together
to create this grand farce.
A myriad of nonsense
As preposterous as Tarot or astrology.
You're not listening,
Listen to me! . . . You're not listening, Ahh!

Voltaire: They never met

Richelieu: Who never met?

Voltaire: Galileo, Newton, Descartes, they never met. Well, Newton and Leibnitz did meet briefly, but they had different systems. Different ways of looking at things.

Richelieu: Different rooms in the same house. They all propose belief in things I can't see or touch or smell. Invisible things (*gesturing in the air*) that operate all around me, pushing and pulling, spinning and falling. Makes me dizzy. And when I ask you to explain, you refer me to some gibberish, scrolled on scraps of paper, in the library of some recluse in England or in Italy. If you are searching for what is real, I'll tell you what is real. Having to feed ten thousand troops and their camp followers in the middle of winter, in the middle of nowhere. That's real! That's about as real as you can get.

Voltaire: And then some

Richelieu: The question remains, why?

Voltaire: Don't start that again.

Richelieu: Why would you pass up all of the opportunities that are before us? What has changed? Why sacrifice everything for the love of one woman when there are so many who are so healthy and willing and needing love?

Voltaire: Yes, yes, yes … all of that is true. I don't know what has changed really, but I see things differently now. Emilie has had a profound effect on my psyche. And she is wonderful! She is a woman who has jeopardized everything for me. This is someone who is always there. She is a treasure most blessed by the Gods. As precious as the snow, the sun the moon and the stars. Besides the fact that she is one of a handful of people in the world who understand 'the system'.

Richelieu: Emilie has her own responsibilities. A family and position to think of. I cannot believe I did not see this coming.

(*The music to the song "Emilie" begins in the background*)

Voltaire: It wasn't really anything you would have noticed at all. It all changed rather quickly. Last winter at the masked ball—

(Voltaire begins the song Emilie)

'Emilie'

She came crashing through my life
Like a flash in a breeze, in a summer sky.
In the circus of our Parisian nightlife,
She was staring at me.
But what even shocked me more,
after walking across that salon floor,
Is that I followed her to her coach
And that coach took me home.
Sometimes, you're in a world of your own.
Then someone comes along,
And steals your heart with their eyes,
their sighs, their dreams, their mind.
Sometimes, you're so caught up in your rut,
when too much is not enough,
to make you feel alive, she finds your eyes one night.
With a soul as vast as the sea,
It's no mystery why I am with Emilie.
Emilie smiles and lights up my soul,
Emilie, so young yet a thousand years old.
It was always there,
and I didn't know it
Took an angel to show me the jewel in the lotus.
It was always there and I didn't know it
Took an angel to show me the jewel in the lotus.
It was always there, it was always there.

(Emilie and Maupertuis enter the room.)

Emilie: Francois, Maurpertuis has agreed to help us. He will make our case in Paris, explaining all that we are trying to do. To the authorities and the academe … and my family!

Voltaire: And the Duc has agreed to do the same at court and to Florent-Claude, that is, I think he will—

Richelieu: yes, yes of course he will.

Voltaire: Then we are all in agreement!

Emilie: So, there it is! We will make it so! I love you all!

(The four of them join hands, raising them above their heads)

All four in unison: "We will stand together … all as one!"

The Curtain Falls

Scene Two

(The curtain opens to a cutout of Emilie and Voltaire's rooms upstage. Emilie's room, on the left is decorated in yellow with light blue trim. The window curtains are woven tapestries. There is a canopy bed, framed with dark blue curtains. There are several Wattau sketches on the walls. She is seated at her desk in the middle of the room. Voltaire's room is like an alchemist's study, with bookshelves, globes, and a writing desk with several large books open on it. He also has a canopy bed with the curtains drawn. He is sitting on it with books scattered about, in his bed cap and nightgown. A chambermaid is running back and forth with notes and messages from the two. There is laughter at the receipt of each note by Voltaire and Emilie. The maid is becoming tired and winded from running back and forth. The more tired and frustrated she becomes, the louder the opening and closing of the door becomes. Emilie, writing as she speaks her lines and Voltaire following suit)

Emilie: So what have you in mind for our next play?

Voltaire: I have been concocting a comedy.

Emilie: I was hoping for a tragedy, I've been feeling rather heroic of late.

Voltaire: No, something lite … a spoof on the love intrigues at court. You know, screw Richelieu . . . pump Pompadour, Louie's louie, Orleans slong. Something along those lines.

Emilie: Ah, yes! And I can see us dashing for the border, in the middle of the night, in the snow, as the police close in on us … You must be getting bored.

Voltaire: I can't help it. These things just pop into my head.

Emilie: Why cause trouble?

Voltaire: It is just for our little theater. No one outside of our troupe will even know of its existence. A little jewel, briefly put on display.

Emile: Versailles has ears everywhere. It is amazing. I suspect that De Graffigny is sending an entire gazette to that little jackal De Croy. My maid tells me that she was taking notes at your last reading from Joan of Arc. Should I catch her —

Voltaire: There! That proves it; that was weeks ago and nothing has come of it. We will never get anything done if we're always looking over our shoulders. The bogeymen are days away in Paris. Relax. We built this place so that we could have the intellectual freedom to express these things. It would be a shame if we went to all that trouble only to be afraid to enjoy its fruits.

(Down stage Richelieu hurriedly enters the salon and speaks to Jeannine, Emilie's maid. Hearing the commotion Longchamp rushes in. Jeannine takes Richelieu's coat and excitedly runs to Longchamp to tell him the news. They both leave to tell Emilie and Voltaire what is happening. The maid is hysterical as she speaks to Emilie.)

(Longchamp tells Voltaire the news. He listens intently, making decisions. Both scenes are woven together.)

Emilie: Jeannine what's wrong? Is that the Marchal's coat? Is he here? Calm down, speak slowly.

Jeannine: Madame, they are coming to arrest you! No, no, no not you, M. Voltaire. They are coming to arrest M. Voltaire!

Longchamp: Frankly sir, we have no other choice.

Voltaire: Yes, yes, make the coach ready just in case. Thank you, Sebastian, for everything. *(shaking his hand)* Is Richelieu in the parlor?

Longchamp: Yes sir, he is waiting there to speak to you both.

(*He puts on his robe to meet Richelieu. Emilie is doing the same*)

Emilie: Please tell the Duc Richelieu that I will be there shortly.

Jeannine: Yes mam. (*leaving*)

(*Voltaire and Emilie both leave their rooms at the same time and meet in the hallway. They join hands and go to meet Richelieu in the parlor*)

Richelieu: Ahh! Finally. Sit down, both of you. I have things to tell you. It's serious this time. Your "English letters" are being read in every salon and parlor in Paris. The censors are furious. They want your head. The King's ministers are saying it is treasonous. They claim that the anti-French sentiments in it are proof that you are an agent of the English. On top of that, there are sections of a work about Joan of Arc that are being circulated, attributed to you and they are saying it is sacrilege. The clergy are claiming that it proves that you are an atheist. Everyone is up in arms. They are accusing you of trying to corrupt society.

(*Emilie and Voltaire look at each other and speak at the same time*)

Emilie : De Graffigny !

Voltaire: De Graffigny!

Richelieu: The Prefect of Police already has a warrant for your arrest. It has been on his desk for over a year. Now he has his excuse. The Queen is angry at both of you for allowing this to happen. The King is very annoyed! You are interrupting the entertainments at court. The Prefects agents are sure to be on their way. This weather slowed me down considerably. It took forever to get here, and it will slow them down as well.

Actually, it is a blessing. It will give us some time to get you safely away.

Voltaire: Maybe they will make a wrong turn and get lost in the snow. And Emilie? Is she safe from this?

Richelieu: She is not being brought into the matter. They are looking past their own, so to speak. This is all about you!

Emilie: *(angrily)* When I see that little muckraker —

Voltaire: In time Emilie, *(to Richelieu)* Longchamp is getting the coach ready. I just have to pack a few things —

Richelieu: No, no time for that!
(the maid comes in with a bag of food)
I've had some things made ready for you and you must leave immediately.

Jeannine: I put in a couple of bottles of your favorite wine Mssr. *(she curtsies)*

Voltaire: Thank you Jeannine, you are an angel.

(Longchamp enters)

Longchamp: The coach is ready sir. The driver says he knows of a shortcut through the forest that will get us to the border in good time.

(Emilie brings Voltaire his overcoat and puts it on his shoulders)

Voltaire: I can't leave in my bedclothes!

Longchamp: I have taken the liberty of choosing a few things to take with you, Mssr. They are in the coach.

Richelieu: This is no time for talk.

Emilie: As soon as you are safely across the border you must write me to tell me where you are.

Richelieu: That's not such a good Idea. The mail will surely be intercepted and read. We must be very careful.

Voltaire: *(to Emilie)* Everything will be fine! Don't worry. This is not the first time I have had to escape. One time I hid in plain sight at Richelieu's military camp, while the prefects henchmen chased all over France looking for me. *(Richelieu laughs, then collects himself)*

Richelieu: Let's go. This is no time for long stories. Precious time is being wasted!

Longchamp: The carriage is waiting sir.

(Voltaire hugs Emilie and Richelieu, and leaves with Longchamp)

Voltaire: Sebastian, we have to come up with a new identity for me. Something original, something with panache!

(Emilie hugs Richelieu, turning to see Voltaire as he passes through the door.)

Richelieu: Just as he said, he has been through this before. *(She embraces Richelieu, the maid is crying)* And I suspect this will not be the last time.

The Curtain Falls

Act III

Scene One

(Next morning M.Maupertuis, M.Algorotti, Mme De Graffigny, two women guest and a gentleman neighbor are in the salon at Cirey. They stand before a great window, conversing, overlooking the estate. It is snowing. A maid is preparing the morning coffee at a side table).

<u>Gentleman:</u> When do you leave for your Lapland expedition, Monsieur?

<u>Maupertuis:</u> The preparations are being taken care of as we speak. That should place our departure at about two months from now.

<u>Lady1:</u> How exciting.

<u>De Graffigny:</u> I don't understand.

Lady1: It's about the Englishman Newton. Something about measuring a bulge.

De Graffigny: You mean like measuring a waistline.

Maupertuis: Actually, that is exactly correct Madame. (*to the gentleman*) Out of the mouths of children. . . . It is of course far more complicated than Madame's analogy. I am one of the few people in the world that is capable of carrying out this experiment. It will be a triumph for science.

Gentleman: (sarcastically) As it has for dress makers for all of time.(*all laugh except Maupertuis*)

Lady2: It seems very quiet around here without M Voltaire. He is always very animated during our morning coffee.

Maupertuis: He thrives on drama.

Lady2: Then his wish has been fulfilled! (*raising her coffee cup*)

Maupertuis: Voltaire has become a bore. (*with a salty smile*)

De Graffigny: And she, she talks about things I can't understand.

Maupertuis: Madam, to explain anything to you would be a challenge for anyone.

De Graffigny: What kind of people invite you to their home, give you coffee and cakes in the morning then disappear for the rest of the day . . . until dinner! And then at dinner you are expected to be as animated and well informed as they are.

Maupertuis: I'm sure that would be challenging for you Madam. (*feigning sympathy*)

Lady2: It was amazing! The other night she was reading aloud to us in French, a text written in Latin. I was able to watch her work through the translation and the calculations in her mind as she was reading it to us. It was amazing! That is just how fast she is!

Algoratti: Voltaire only speaks of his pet projects. Constantly! They become less interesting each time. On the other hand, Madam! She is incredible when it comes to calculations. I know firsthand, as I am her tutor.

Lady2: (*playing the coquette*) A reflection upon her illustrious teacher, no doubt.

Algoratti: (*returning her flirtation*) Madam is too kind. Perhaps, should you find time, I would like to show you some things.

Lady2: It is the duty of every noblewoman to show the warmest hospitality to our famous guest whilst they visit us. (*Algoratti kisses her hand. Richelieu's music is heard as he enters the room*)

Richelieu: Good morning, everyone. (*kissing hands and greeting everyone*)

Maupertuis: Morning, monsieur.

Algoratti: Monsieur.

(*the ladies curtsy coquettishly*)

Lady1:Monsieur.

Lady2: Monsieur.

Richelieu: Look at that snow! It's looks as though I made it here just in time. The roads were terrible last night. (*maid brings him coffee*)

Lady1: The snow is very beautiful.

Richelieu: Not for all I'm afraid, Madam.

Maupertuis: A slight inconvenience in the Lapland

Algoratti: Any word from our host monsieur?

Richelieu: No, no word yet. Hopefully he has made it to the border and is warming himself by a roaring fire.

Maupertuis: Drama, drama

Lady1: Should not M Voltaire have waited for the king's officers? (*they all roll their eyes*)

Richelieu: Of course madam, as an officer of the King myself, (*eyeing De Gaffiginy*) I tried to detain him but somehow he slipped out of my custody. Were it not for the weather, I would be in hot pursuit, of course.

All: of course

Richelieu: I am sure it is all a misunderstanding and all will return to normal in a little while.

Maupertuis: (*sarcastically*) Perhaps by the time I return from Lapland….

(*Richelieu has had his eye on a young maid who has come into the room making busy work for herself. Richelieu has become distracted. The ladies in the group are put off by the loss of Richelieu's attention as the men smile to each other in approval*)

Maupertuis: If all goes well, (*not missing a beat*) I should return within a year's time. Every leg of the journey has been meticulously planned.

(*Algoratti and Lady2 have slipped off to the side and are quietly talking. Richelieu takes the opportunity to get close to the young maid who is dusting on the other side of the room. Only Maupertuis, De Graffigny and Lady1 are left. Maupertuis acts as though he does not notice any change and continues.*)

Maupertuis: The academe has been very generous in their funding. Of course, understanding the importance of my findings.

De Graffigny & Lady1: Of course! (*smiling at each other*)

Richelieu:(*to the maid*) I would like some more coffee if you please Annie.

Annie: (*curtsying*) You know my name Monsieur?

Richelieu: Of course. How could I not know the name of such a lovely creature. You are Annie Deveraux. You have lived your entire life in the village of Cirey. Your father works at the foundry, as did his father. You have been in Madam's employ for six months now, and she is very pleased with your service. (*Annie takes his cup and saucer nervously and runs to the coffee station for a refill. Richelieu stares out of the window at the snow thinking about Voltaire battling the weather.*)

Richelieu: (*to himself*) I hope it's going well for you my *friend* (*Annie returns with the coffee. She is visibly nervous*) But there is so much more about you that I would like to know. What do you say we take a stroll and you can tell me everything about yourself.

Annie: But it's snowing Monsieur.!

Richelieu: Bah! What I see is ever lasting spring, and it's wonderful!

(*slowly walking her towards the garden doors*)

Pegasus

Come take a walk,
down through this garden with me.
<u>*Annie:*</u> *But it's snowing Monsieur.*
I've got something to tell you.
It won't take long,
No longer than a song takes
To tell you how I feel
<u>*Annie:*</u> *But it's snowing Monsieur.*
I've taken Pegasus, right from Zeus's stables
And he's carried me clear across the sky.
I found the stars of the night
Deep in your eyes,
And I want you in my life.

(*Emilie appears at the doorway, calmly giving instructions to a servant. Richelieu, anticipating the coming drama, takes the maid by the hand and escapes through the doors into the garden. Emilie storms into the room refusing the approach of the maid carrying her coffee. She walks directly to De Graffigny as Maupertuis and Lady1 slide away to the coffee station to observe.*)

<u>Emilie:</u> (*hands on her hips*) How could you? Do you know what you have done? Why would you do this? You take a simple night's entertainment, something private, and turn it into a controversy! (*pacing*) Monsieur Voltaire reads some little amusement for everyone's pleasure and within a week it is a scandal in Paris! Where do you keep your couriers? Where are they hiding? How do you do this? (*pacing*)

<u>Maupertuis:</u> (*to lady1*) I'd be surprised if she understands at all.

<u>De Graffigny:</u> Madam, I am sure I don't understand. (sobbing)

Emilie: I bring you into my home, show you the hospitality of Cirey and this is how you thank me.

De Graffigny: Madam you are being horrible (*crying*) You have ignored me since I arrived. My room is cold and damp. The wind blows through so strongly it blows the candles out.

Emilie: (*to her maid*) Please see that Gerard looks to Madam De Graffigny's rooms.

De Graffigny: And there is nothing else to do all day but to write letters and sleep. (*still crying*) You should be more kind to your guest.

Emilie: Guest! More like a spy! When the weather clears and the roads are passable Madam, I would like you to pack your bags and leave!

(*she turns her back on De Graffigny and steps up to the window. Her maid brings her coffee. De Graffigny joins the others at the coffee station, kerchief in hand, drying her eyes while sipping her coffee. All eyes are on Emilie. At the window watching the snow she begins her song.*)

Light From My Window

The light from my window, dances on the rug.
It turns my thoughts to the love we share.
And its growing,
I think its showing.
There's part of your voice
still floating about the room. Your shadows still here,
it laughs and swears that you'll be back home soon.
To hold me, I know
Your shadow told me.
Sometimes we're so close; it feels we're far apart.
If memory serves correctly, I knew that from the start.
From the moment that you came into my heart,
There's this wondrous music, this calling from afar.
Come and shine your light on me
Come and shine your light on me.
Come and shine your light on, come and shine your light on me.

(While Emilie finishes her song the butler enters the salon with a tray of letters on it. He looks about the room for the Duc Richelieu. Not seeing him, he asks the maid where the Duc might be. She points to the doors that open to the garden and the butler marches through. Richelieu and the maid reenter the room adjusting their clothes. The butler points to Emilie,l standing at the window. Richelieu joins her. The butler admonishes the maid as they leave the room.)

<u>Richelieu:</u> I have word from Longchamp. He has sent two messages. The first to say that they have arrived safely at the border and are traveling incognito. The second letter to say they have settled comfortably in Geneva and are doing well. They are very busy visiting local dignitaries and the town's

leading men, hmm, even receiving a standing ovation at the theater.

Emilie: (*sarcastically*) I was just envisioning him trudging through the snow, nobly suffering for his art. Instead, I learn he is enjoying a new celebrity. I never know what to expect from him. Everything is constantly changing. He is like an amorphous cloud. He has a charmed life my urchin does! He turns misfortune to his advantage. I never know what to expect.

Richelieu: Mon Cher, what we should expect from Francois is the unexpected!

(*An evening scrim drops down darkening the stage, leaving only a silhouette of Emilie. An inter-mezzo is played.*

The scrim rises and there is daylight again. Emilie at the window is still a silhouette, not noticed as people mill about the room doing their days business.

The evening scrim lowers again leaving only the silhouette of Emilie

(*Voltaire's waltz is played slowly*)

End of Scene One

Scene Two

(The curtain opens to the salon; it is spring. Voltaire is seen standing at the window, gazing out upon the flowering dogwood trees. Emilie has entered the room . She sees Voltaire at the window and rushes to him, arms open. They hug for a while, laughing and sighing, Emilie is crying).

Emilie: *(wiping her eyes)* My renegade vagabond! You don't look any the worse for your troubles. *(Holding his face in her hands)* At first I was so worried . . . then *(pacing)* Longchamp sent word that you had become a celebrity in Geneva! While I have been stuck here, snowbound and distracted, you were attending dinners held in your honor. Cirey is not the same when you are not here Francois. It needs you to bring it to life.

(Emilie goes to the coffee bar to fetch coffee for them both)

Voltaire: Emilie, you are the life blood of this place. I am just a part of its décor . . .A trophy on the wall!

Emilie: There were times this past winter when I would have loved to hang your head on the wall.

Voltaire: *(laughing)* I could feel it even at a great distance.

Emilie: Yours was not the only head I would have hung there, but your place was reserved.....dead center . . . surrounded by your obsequious sycophants.

Voltaire: I think my head would look fetching above fireplace.

Emilie: Of course . . . the focal point . . . when one enters the room there you are! . . . opportunist!

Voltaire: But an opportunist who is crazy about you! Has the Duc arrived yet?

Emilie: I didn't know he was coming. He comes and goes for a few days at a time. Mm Pompadour has taken for herself the duties of master of entertainment. I think he comes here to soothe his pride.

Voltaire: He has held that position for quite a while now . . . helped me back into the good graces of the king with that little play Rameau and I put together.

Emilie: Ach! *(disapprovingly)*

Voltaire: It was the music! It was a perfectly good play! . . . that awful music ruined it.

Emilie: The king's favorite part of the production.

Voltaire: We both know the King has horrible taste!

Emilie: Of course *(sarcastically)*

Voltaire: Of course! *(returning his cup to the coffee station)* Emilie . . . that's it! That's what we'll do. We will stage a play! A musical!

Emilie: That's a wonderful idea! Something where I can sing (pirouetting) sing away the doldrums of this past winter.

(The music for 'Time to put on a play' starts in the background.)

'Time To Put On A Play'

Voltaire: It's time to put on a play.
It's time to put on our costumes and say outrageous things,
that only thespians can say!
It's time to put on a play,
so call out the servants,
light the stage.
We'll do something exotic,
about some far-off distant place

Emilie: I'll play a princess, a damsel in distress! (sic)

Voltaire; And I'll will come to your rescue and save your ass....(laughing)

Together: It's time to put on a play!

(Voltaire takes Emilie's hands and they begin dancing in circles about the room)

Voltaire: Dance with me Emilie! Dance like you've never danced before!

Emilie: Will I be seeing some of Mssr. Arouets famous fancy footwork?

Voltaire: Only my best ! . . . Dance Emilie, dance with me. There are things that can only be said in a delicious Terpsichore.

(Voltaire releases Emilie's hand and she pirouettes across the room.)

Voltaire: Dance with your shadow!

Emilie: Sing with your echo!

(A melody of previous songs is played as they dance; sometimes together, sometimes solo. "Voltaire's waltz" begins, followed by "what have you heard" as a primitive drum song with Emilie

intimating a tribal a dance.. Richelieu appears in the salon doorway. He is smiling at the sight of Emilie and Voltaire dancing and laughing. The music of Richelieu's Waltz is played as Richelieu enters the room.)

Richelieu: If only Paris could see you now! Greetings friends, it's so good to see you both happy! *(music ends)* Perfect timing! Coming from the doldrums of Paris, you both are a sight for sore eyes. *(pours himself a glass of wine)* At times I understand your self-imposed exile . . . *(catching himself)* or whatever you call it. It's so good to be here.

Voltaire: Perfect indeed! We are going to put on a play. A play with music! With your experience staging Fetes for the court and our creativity we shall create the best show in the land!

(Richelieu puts his wine glass down, pacing, hand on his chin)

Richelieu: *(to himself)* Hum. . . . I could surely find at least a quartet of musicians . . . Troupes of actors are always available . . . *(turning to Emilie and Voltaire)* and I know the most wonderful seamstress in the Maris who is an excellent costume maker. She can make anything we ask her to.

(Emilie and Voltaire smile at each other knowing Richelieu is now committed to the project. Richelieu continues as though taking over the project.)

Richelieu: This has to be good, . . . it has to remind the King of what he has been missing since the "Maitresse Du Roi" has taken over our amusements at court! *(pouring himself another drink)* Tell me what you need and I will make the arrangements. . . . *(empties his glass)* I shall treat this as a military campaign, . . . We must outdo Pompadour!

Emilie: We need you on the stage!

Richelieu: You know I don't do that! I am a military man!

Voltaire: Would be a big draw--

Emilie: Who is also an "Impresario" as flamboyant as they come.

Voltaire; Now I'm thinking we might not be able to accommodate a great number of people.

Emilie: *(to Voltaire)* Later ... just a detail.

Richelieu: *(To Voltaire))* Stay focused. . . . Concentrate on the show.

Voltaire: Emilie, I could take the songs you have been working on lately and weave a story line...follow it wherever it goes.

Emilie: I have a couple that might work. I will see to the decorations of course. (*to herself sarcastically*) And the menu, the guest list and the seating arrangements. *(She sticks her tongue out at Voltaire)*

Richelieu: We have much to do, . . . this show must be stellar! Something to be talked about for months. We must outdo Pompadour! This is a military campaign like no other! We must out do Pompadour!

Together: (joining *raised hands*) Outdo Pompadour!

End of Scene Two

Scene Three

*(The curtain opens to a theater with a stage set in the back. The stage is framed by Greek mythological characters and at the crown a banner reading **Theatre Du Cirey.***

The chairs are laid out in typical semi-circle fashion separated by an aisle. Voltaire is huddled with designers and carpenters at the foot of the stage, working out the details of the stage sets. Emilie is busy placing flowers and the candelabra that will light the stage.)

Emilie: *(To the workmen)* The light should never leave me when I am on stage. *(moving closer to the stage)* You! Not that close to the curtains! We don't want to burn the house down. *(Laughing, turning to the candle foreman beside her)* We should have a cluster of lights here, at the foot of the stage. When I need to, I can step into the light.

Voltaire: *(to the stage crew with him on stage)* The actors must have room to move around, . . . too much furniture can make for embarrassing moments. Color is most important Henri.

(There are workmen milling about, everyone with a task as Richelieu and an actress enter stage right arranging their clothes)

Richelieu: You spoke your lines excellently! I will definitely speak to Francois and let him know just how well you performed. *(Grinning, Richelieu, with giant steps crosses over to a group of men on the far end of the room)* Gentlemen! I am so sorry to have kept you waiting *(shaking hands)* there are a thousand details to attend to and I am no longer in control of my time. Sooo . . . right where we are standing, I would like to set up our little orchestra. That will give us plenty of room, with more light coming from the window, and a clear view of the stage. Sooo . . . if you set up your seating arrangement here, we will be ready to go. That would be wonderful! Thank you so much! *(Seeing a mixed group of troupe players across the room, Richelieu goosesteps over to greet them)*

Richelieu: Good people! You are the first people I should have addressed *(shaking hands)*. Everyone knows that the troupe players are the backbone of any show! Welcome to you all! Mssr. Voltaire will fill you in with the details of the parts you are to play and where you will be placed. In all matters of the stage I will be deferring to Mssr. Voltaire and the Marquise.

Their decisions are to be considered final. Please . . . no temper tantrums this time people!

(Voltaire on stage, clapping his hands, calling the troupe to him)

Voltaire: OK, let's get this started. Gather round. . . . Women on the left, . . . Men on the right if you please. *(placing himself in the middle)*
What we are trying to create here is . . .

(Scrim falls, an intermezzo is played. Scrim rises again to Emilie and Voltaire at the foot of center stage. Emilie's maid joins them.)

Jeannine: The roads are very crowded and more than half of the guests will be arriving late. The staff is concerned that they may not be able to accommodate a group as large as what we are seeing. We need to know what Madam wants to do.

Voltaire: (Sarcastically) A detail! (Richelieu *enters and seeing the look on Emilie's and Voltaire's face reassures them*)

Richelieu: Not to worry. . . . All is well...I have had my people sequester temporary housing down the road from here. Just beyond the gardens by the river. Fully equipped! Better than home for some. Focus on the show.

Curtain Falls

(The curtain rises to a packed house. The orchestra is warming up. There is a lot of commotion from behind the curtain . The audience is jovial, willing to wait for the last minute changes to be put in place. The din of the chattering audience subsides as Voltaire steps from behind the stage curtain and crosses to the footlights.)

Voltaire: Ladies and Gentlemen. Welcome to our little theater at Cirey. Coming here has been a long journey for you, and we have worked hard to present to you something worthy of your effort and enterprise. We have assembled the finest players to be found in the entire region and their only wish is to put a smile on all of your faces.

Ladies and Gentlemen . . . our players!

(*Stage Curtain Rises***)**

(The cast comes on stage from all quarters, dances and sings. "It's time to put on a show". The cast dances before a backdrop of Cirey. Standard boy-girl back and forth choreography. They finish their number and fade into the background. Voltaire returns to the footlights clapping enthusiastically.)

Voltaire: Wonderful . . . that was wonderful! Ladies and Gentleman may I introduce to you Madam Emilie Bretuile du Chatelet. *(Emilie enters stage right, humming the theme playing in the background)*

Emilie: Good evening Francois.

Voltaire: Good evening Emilie

(Emilie, center stage begins her song)

Mountain Stream of Dreams

Mountain stream of dreams flowing by,
sit back, relax, cause you've arrived, . . . in Paradise.
Flowers line her banks,
She meanders on and on and on,
through Paradise!

(Voltaire crosses to center stage to join Emilie)

Voltaire: Walking down this road on this starry evening.

Emilie: Watching rivers flow, above and below.

Voltaire: You've got to dance with your shadow

Emilie: Sing with your echo

(They dance a short Fandango)

Emilie: Take another look...fall in love with your lover

Voltaire: Throw the moon a kiss

Together: Take time to love each other.

Voltaire: Dance with your shadow,

Emilie: Sing with your echo.

(They dance a short Fandango)

Emilie: Mt stream of dreams, flowing by.

So rich in color, a banquet for the eyes...in Paradise.
Cloud castles drifting by, it's so incredible the depth and the blues
of the sky . . . in Paradise

Voltaire: Walking down this road, on this starry evening.

Emilie: Watching rivers flow, above and below.

Voltaire: You've got to dance with your shadow,

Emilie: Sing with your echo.

(They dance the Fandango)

Emilie: Take another look, fall in love with your lover
Voltaire: Throw the moon a kiss
Together: Take time to love each other
Voltaire: Dance with your shadow
Emilie: Sing with your echo

(A short Fandango is danced again. Voltaire bows to Emilie and returns to the footlights clapping and encouraging the audience to give a big round of applause. Emilie bows and exits stage left.)
Voltaire: An amazingly talented person! Ladies and Gentlemen Emilie du Chatelet!

Now for our next bit of entertainment---

(a chorus of children enter stage right singing)

With Imagination

Children:
With imagination
you can do it all.
With imagination we create the world.
With imagination you are big or small
Let imagination sing all day long,
La la la la la la la la la la la la la lah

(Emilie has entered with the last of the children).

Emilie: Find yourself a river flowing through the trees.

Voltaire: Feel its precious waters tingling at your knees.

Emilie: See the light dancing, laughing as it sings

<u>Together:</u> *Remember, remember, remember!*
       You're part of "Everything"

(Repeat of " With Imagination" by the children as they exit stage left. Emilie follows the last child turning to wave goodbye to the audience. Voltaire returns to the footlights as the audience applauds enthusiastically.)

<u>Voltaire:</u> My friends, that was the children's chorus of the Village of Cirey. They have arranged this piece all on their own . . . well for the most part, ah hum,*(as an aside, hand to his mouth)* with the help of the Marquise, who is their sponsor of course. They perform a most wonderful Christmas concert every year and these our cherubs have been singing since they could walk. Next on stage we have for you, our dancers! Renown throughout France as the premier acrobatic dance troupe. They have prepared a montage of musical numbers that we love to sing here, and we hope you will enjoy it and maybe sing along.

(The troupe dances before changing scenery that rolls by, providing a back drop for each number. They finish, form a tableau, bow and exit the stage.)

<u>Voltaire:</u> *(clapping)* That was something. I'm still dizzy from watching them fly through the air. Incredible! And now, to close the first half of our program we will sing one of our favorite songs here at Cirey . . . *A little bit of heaven.* After that, a sumptuous meal awaits us in the dining room. Ladies and gentlemen, our players!

(The troop fills the stage singing 'Little bit of heaven')

Little Bit of Heaven

There's a little bit of heaven
out there waiting for us all.
A little bit of heaven,
standing just outside the door.
Get yourself together
and go marching right on through.
If it's all there for me,
then it's all there for you!
There's a little bit of heaven,
shining from that distant star.
A little bit of heaven,
just as close as you are.
It's all been given to us,
and ain't that rather grand?
The Marquise, the playwright
And their merry little band!

(The audience stands and applauds. The curtain comes down on the play within a play. Voltaire steps from behind the curtain, walks to the footlights and addresses the live audience.)

Voltaire: Well, hello again. After that we had a fine dinner and resumed our program. That's pretty much what life was like at Cirey, for a couple of years, so that's where I'll leave off. Eventually I went to Prussia and Emilie went with Saint-Lambert, but that's another story for another day. I hope you have enjoyed this slice of life, this vignette of a wonderful time and place. Please come back soon. (bowing) Thank you, a bientot!

Main Curtain Drops

Thank you for Reading Three Plays

Please post a review on Amazon

Other books by Walter E. Ledwith

Acknowledgements

Thank you to the Writer's Windowpane critique group
for all their help and support.

.

www.ingramcontent.com/pod-product-compliance
Lightning Source LLC
Chambersburg PA
CBHW060428260626
47161CB00005B/1828